Advantage

The "A" Word Romances, Volume 2

Jerusha Moors

Published by Sunday Morning Publishing, 2016.

This is a work of fiction. Similarities to real people, places, or events are entirely coincidental.

ADVANTAGE

First edition. July 6, 2016.

Copyright © 2016 Jerusha Moors.

ISBN: 979-8201255770

Written by Jerusha Moors.

Chapter One

A loud clap of thunder jarred Eleanor awake, just as she had finally drifted off to sleep once more. She did not sleep well alone in the manse. Once every creak, every whisper of noise had come from the comforting companionship of her father. Now he had passed, those sounds took on a more ominous feel and exacerbated her already unsteady nerves.

She jumped as a loud bang came from downstairs. It was probably the cat, but Eleanor lay tense, holding her breath as she waited for another sound to disturb the silence in the house. Outside, the wind was howling, and intermittent claps of thunder broke through the splash of the rain. It was a night not fit for man or beast.

Another bang and a yowl told her it was indeed the cat prowling downstairs. Eleanor let out the breath she had been holding while she debated the merits of going back downstairs to see what the filthy animal was doing. Lucifer was her father's pet, named for the angel before his fall though Eleanor thought Beelzebub was a more fitting appellation. The creature missed his lost master and had not ceased prowling about the house, looking for him.

With a muttered blasphemy, Eleanor threw back her covers and arose from her bed. She fumbled with the candle on her nightstand, at last relighting it, then threw on her robe. The floor was cold beneath her feet, and she hoped that she could find the cat quickly and settle him in her father's room. She could make a bed from her father's robe for Lucifer; perhaps that would appease him.

The storm seemed louder as she went out into the hallway. The manse was old, and wind found its way through cracks she never could caulk as well as she liked. Sourton was on the edge of Dartmoor and blasts of air blew across the flat plains and bogs. Eleanor thought most of them aimed directly at the manse. The house never heated well in winter.

Just as she reached the top of the narrow staircase, several things happened: one of those gusts of air blew her candle out, and there was a bolt of lightning that sizzled through the air outside the window. A tremendous cracking noise came from the back of the house near her bedroom, and Eleanor turned just in time to see the giant oak in the rear yard crash through the roof, demolishing her room. Branches and debris poured down on her and actual rain since there was a gaping hole in the ceiling.

Eleanor stepped back, forgetting the stairs, and her foot went out into space. She balanced for just a moment, scrabbling at the walls and struggling not to fall, but another gust of wind roared through the open roof, drenching her with rain and pushing her backward. She wrapped her hands around her head to protect herself as her body smashed down the stairs and then she knew no more.

"MISS ELEANOR, PLEASE wake up dear. Oh, Rawlings, what shall we do? Her father gone just a week past, and now his daughter to follow. This cannot be."

Eleanor didn't open her eyes, trying to get her bearings. Her body throbbed, especially her left leg. Her wet nightdress clung to her body though she couldn't imagine why the life of her. She knew voice though; that was Mrs. Makepeace, the housekeeper from Wykeham Hall, but why she should fret over Eleanor, she didn't know, and her head hurt too much to bother trying to make sense of it.

Slowly she peeled her eyelids open someone thrust a vial of vinegar under her nose. Eleanor coughed which aggravated the pain in her leg and head and made her eyes water.

"Thank the Lord! Rawlings, look, she's alive," Mrs. Makepeace corked the small bottle to Eleanor's relief and took Eleanor's hand.

"I see, Mrs. Makepeace. The lass was breathing after all." At an indignant look from the housekeeper, Mr. Rawlings, for it was he standing to the side of Mrs. Makepeace, hastily tried to placate her. "I knew you would bring her around. With the doctor away in Bath, you were the first person I thought of when I found her this morning."

"What happened?" Eleanor croaked, her throat dry as she tried to swallow. "May I have a glass of water?"

Mr. Rawlings nodded. "Let me step over to the Highwayman and get you some ale. I expect that will clear your whistle."

"Yes, yes, an excellent idea," Mrs. Makepeace pursed her lips, "and perhaps one for myself, too. This has been a dreadful shock to us all."

Eleanor struggled to sit up but subsided when Mrs. Makepeace put a hand on her shoulder. "I wouldn't try to move just yet, Miss Mortimer. You've had a dreadful shock."

"I don't understand what's happened," Eleanor said plaintively. "And water is just fine for me."

"Yes, well, we can't get into your kitchen right now. Ale will have to do."

Eleanor had tracked Mr. Rawlings, the proprietor of the local inn, as he left to get the ale. Her brain felt like someone had stuffed it with cotton-wool and ached as much as the rest of her body. Why were Mr. Rawlings and Mrs. Makepeace in her front room and why couldn't they get into the kitchen? What had happened here?

Lucifer decided that now was a good time to jump on her sore body. Eleanor jumped and screamed as she wrenched her left knee, almost falling off the sofa. Mrs. Makepeace grabbed her just in time.

Seeing the cat reminded her of the night before. She had got out of bed to see what the cat was doing when — Eleanor shivered as she remembered — a tree had come through the roof and then she fell down the front stairs. Lucifer stared at her balefully from the back of the sofa and meowed, reminding her she had not given him his dish of milk yet for the day. Wait, they couldn't get into the kitchen. Eleanor's mind whirled. What did that mean?

"Now don't you worry, Miss Mortimer." Mrs. Makepeace patted her hand, trying to calm her. "I'm sure the new Lord will have the house fixed before you know it."

That thought just added to Eleanor's panic, but before she could ask, Mr. Rawlings walked back in, holding a mug in each hand. He waited until the housekeeper helped Eleanor sit up against some cushions. Every part of her body hurt, but she took the cup and wet her lips with the ale. It was refreshing, and Eleanor took a bigger sip. Mr. Rawlings handed the other one to Mrs. Makepeace, and that good lady took a big gulp of her drink.

"My poor Miss Mortimer," Mr. Rawlings said after both women had finished their ale. "I believe the drink helped. You don't look as pale as you did when I found you."

"Thank you, Mr. Rawlings. I believe you're right." Eleanor handed her empty mug back to the innkeeper. "I remember the storm and the tree coming down, but after that..." She wrung her hands in confusion.

"Why, Miss, that big oak in the back came down right on the back of the house. It's a mercy you weren't in your room, or you might be as dead as your poor father."

Eleanor paled, and Mrs. Makepeace fussed, "Now Mr. Rawlings, that is unnecessary. The poor vicar has only been in the ground a week, and Miss Eleanor is still becoming accustomed to that sad fact."

Mr. Rawlings looked ashamed, but he lowered his head and continued. "Old Jed came and got me this morning first thing. He was passing and saw the damage from the storm. We came back and found you lying at the bottom of the staircase. Almost stopped my heart, it did. I thought you…" he paused with a look at Mrs. Makepeace, who scowled at him.

"We got you on the sofa here, and Old Jed went to fetch Mrs. Makepeace, the doctor being away."

Mr. Rawlings was a short man, and Old Jed was in his seventies, Eleanor reflected. She was not heavy, but she was a tall woman, and it must have been an effort for the men to lift her and carry her to the couch, with her unconscious.

"I remember hearing a noise that Lucifer was making down here, and I came to see what he was about Just as I reached the top of the stairs, the tree came through the roof, and I lost my balance."

"Well, look at that. Your father reached through from the beyond, so his cat to alert you to the danger." Mr. Rawlings eyed the feline sitting on top of the sofa back with awe. The ginger tabby was licking a part of his anatomy not appropriate for a lady to view.

"Mr. Rawlings!" Mrs. Makepeace was shaking her head and rolling her eyes, failing utterly to be subtle about her rebuke.

Eleanor smiled wanly. "It's all right, Mrs. Makepeace. Who knows? Perhaps it *was* a message from my father." She sighed. "But what am I to do now? How badly is the manse damaged?"

"Oh, miss, you can't stay here. The tree may have caused the initial damage, but the rain has soaked half the house and wrecked everything in the back of the manse. It all has to dry out and then sorted through to see what we can save. That's not even saying how safe the structure might be. This is an old building and has needed repairs for some time. Your father wouldn't allow it; he wanted any extra money to go to the poor of the parish. And the old lord couldn't be bothered even if it was his duty." Mrs. Makepeace sniffed, her opinion of her past employer clear.

Eleanor bit her lip, not wanting to cry in front of her two rescuers. She knew they meant well, but this was all she had left of her father.

His study was in the back of the house next to the kitchen where he could stay warmer. It contained his papers and all of his books. And the painting of her mother. A tear ran down her cheek, and her lip quivered.

"Now, now, Miss, don't you worry." Mrs. Makepeace looked troubled herself which wasn't very reassuring to Eleanor. More tears rolled down her cheeks, and Mr. Rawlings pulled out a slightly dirty handkerchief and handed it to her.

The two good Samaritans waited until Eleanor had a hold of herself once more. One final sniff into the handkerchief, Eleanor handed the messy rag back to its owner who just tucked it back in his pocket.

"Miss Eleanor, we'll take you up to the big house. There's no one there but a few servants, and we can take proper care of you there. You're all banged up, and you've hurt your leg so you can't walk."

"But the new lord —"

"Is nowhere in sight. A Duke has no interest in a small estate like Wykeham and won't bother you. By rights, he should have taken care of the manse after the old lord died, but I suppose he's too busy with all his other estates."

"I don't know if I should stay there. I don't belong."

"Pish!" Mrs. Makepeace was emphatic. "Where else are you going to stay in this small village? You can't stay at the Highwayman, a gentle-born young lady like yourself. There's nowhere else suitable."

Eleanor conceded that the housekeeper was right. The village was small, and while the Highwayman Inn had rooms to rent, it would not be appropriate for her to stay there alone.

"You haven't heard from the new lord, the Duke?" she asked Mrs. Makepeace.

"Not a word. We had one letter months ago from his man of business notifying us that the Duke had inherited Wykeham Hall. He made arrangements with Mr. Brown, the property manager, to have our wages paid. I don't expect him to show up for months if ever."

Eleanor finally conceded. "Then I will come up to the big house to stay until I can make better arrangements."

Mr. Rawlings clapped his hands together. "Let me get the horse and wagon hitched up, and we'll give you a ride up the road."

"And I'll see what I can find in the way of clothing without venturing into a dangerous area of the house." Mrs. Makepeace stood. "You just stay right there until we come back."

Eleanor nodded. "If the tree destroyed my room, you might find a coat or something in my father's room. His bedroom is near the top of the stairs, and I think it escaped most of the damage. That might have to do for now."

"Don't you worry, Miss Mortimer. We'll take care of you. Your father was a good guardian of Sourton, and people here haven't forgotten his kindnesses."

"Thank you both." Eleanor looked at Lucifer as the others went about their errands. The cat had jumped down to nestle on her robe between her feet. He gave her a huge yawn, sharp teeth exposed as his tongue stretched out.

"Well, Lucifer, I expect that you must go with us. As long as the Duke doesn't show up, I guess it will be all right for a short stay. Then we have to decide what to do next."

Chapter Two

James Lennox, Duke of Carlisle, rode along on his gray stallion, Ajax, as they followed the country roads through Devonshire. It was a beautiful day despite the mud and debris left from storms a few nights before. Jamie was glad to exit the carriage and use Ajax for this last part of the long journey.

They had outstripped the carriage soon after leaving the inn where his entourage had stayed last night. Bates would be irate that he had disappeared, but Jamie needed time to himself. Riding for two days stuck inside the coach with his valet was tedious. Not that Jamie minded Bates that much; he was a good fellow, but they didn't have much to talk about together besides the condition of Jamie's clothing.

Jamie wasn't a snob. He might be a Duke, but that didn't mean he thought himself above others. As a Scotsman among the English, thin though that blood might be, Jamie had been tormented throughout his school years. Being a red-head hadn't helped either, even if his hair had lost the coppery brightness of his boyhood and was more of an auburn now. Only when his beloved father had died, and Jamie gained the title, had he gained the grudging respect of his peers.

There were exceptions, of course. Richard Blount, Earl of Wakefield, was a good friend and had stood by his ginger-haired friend at Oxford. Edmund Thornton, before he had passed, had also been a worthy friend. Richard's sister, Lucy, was also a friend of sorts.

Jamie snorted. Once he thought Lucy might be more than a friend. They had always gotten along over the years, Lucy being more of an outcast from society than himself, so they looked out for each other.

That was the other reason that Jamie rode alone and ahead of the rest of his entourage. Now it was time for Jamie to find a wife and beget heirs, and he was at a loss. Despite the English debutantes looking askance at his Scots blood, Jamie was still a Duke and a wealthy one at that. He was reasonably good looking, despite his hair and a slight accent, and many a young woman of the Ton would hold her nose to marry him.

Once a young lady of the Ton had betrayed Jamie, and he was not eager to play the dupe again. He thought he had found a solution in Lucy Blount. She turned down his marriage proposal once, but Jamie believed he could convince her they were friends enough to have a decent marriage together. He didn't know the entire story, but Lucy had also been in love at one time, but her lover betrayed her. She had sworn off marriage despite her brother Richard's attempts to find her a spouse.

Then Aubrey de Vere, Viscount Lovell, had turned up after five years on the Continent. It was apparent to Jamie that Aubrey was Lucy's first lover. After observing the man, Jamie believed de Vere kept his own feelings for Lucy. Whatever had been the issue between them, de Vere determined to resolve it and make Lucy his own once more. Jamie had no hopes as far as Lucy was concerned.

Hence the journey to Wykeham Hall and his introspection this morning. He knew he needed a wife. He had sent a letter to his mama asking for her aid and suggestions. The Dowager Duchess of Carlisle fretted about her only son, and though she didn't say so to him, she wished for grandchildren. Jamie had resigned himself to a loveless marriage, and he trusted his mother to find him a wife who would be a helpmate and a suitable Duchess.

He also had asked her to find a young vicar looking for a new parish. The village of Sourton had recently seen the death of their religious leader. The man had been there for many years from what his agent said, and since the living belonged to Wykeham Hall, it was Jamie's duty to fill the vacancy.

Wykeham Hall was a small estate among his many properties. Jamie had inherited it from an elderly second cousin. His agent said the place hadn't been maintained; the old lord had not been a proper overseer to the estate, and someone needed to put it to rights.

Since Jamie had no reason to be in London at this time, he had decided it time for a visit to the place, assess its needs, and put its affairs in order. That it was also an opportunity for him to be away from observing the progress of Lucy's courtship with de Vere was just a bonus. While he had not been in love with Lucy, Jamie still felt a twinge in his gut she was finding romance while he was always alone. He wished her every happiness, and he would literally kill de Vere if he harmed her in any way, but Jamie felt left behind. Which made him out of sorts from his usual serene demeanor.

Rooftops and trees rose ahead over the moors, and Ajax pricked up his ears. It looked like he had reached the village of Sourton.

Jamie made his way past a few outlying houses, past a stout inn called the Highwayman, a few shops, and other buildings. Some children stopped their play to watch him ride by. Strangers were uncommon in these parts.

The church was near the end of the street. A rickety house stood next to it, shingles turned gray and weathered. It must be the manse of the late vicar, but the last storms had done considerable damage to the building. An old oak had fallen on part of the house, caving in part of the roof and destroying the back section of the place.

Jamie halted Ajax in the street and examined the destruction. It was recent, and it was sizable. As overlord, he did not begrudge the repairs, but they would take time. He'd have to work out what to do with a new vicar until they could complete improvements. He sighed and proceeded onward. It looked like his stay in Devonshire might be longer than he had anticipated.

His agent had said the estate was located about a mile past the village, and Jamie was glad when he spied a low wall and gate marking the grounds. He had not sent ahead to let them know he was coming for a visit. He thought it might be better to catch them unawares so he could make an accurate assessment of the needs of the place. It was possible he might end up selling Wykeham Hall; he had no need of a manor house in a remote part of England.

Ajax walked up the gravel driveway. Puddles marred the surface, indications of lack of attention to maintenance of the grounds. Made of gray stone, not as big as Dalemain, the house was bigger than Jamie had imagined. His late cousin had been a Baron, but he had not been destitute and derived a good income from sheep farming and his tenants. The Baron appeared to have been stingy with his coin and not inclined to reinvest in his home. The closer Jamie got to the house, the better he could see signs of neglect.

Shutters needed paint, and one on the second floor was hanging partly off. The lawn was overgrown, and the outbuildings also required paint. Jamie mentally added more weeks to the length of his stay. He could delegate the overseeing of tasks to his agent, but his father had trained him well. Besides, an extended stay in the country might be just what he needed right now.

He rode Ajax around to what appeared to be the stables and dismounted. He hoped that there was someone still working there; the Baron must have had horses of his own. Sure enough, a tiny old man with a limp hobbled out, shading his eyes from the sun as he adjusted to the light.

"Here now, how can I help ye?" the man asked.

"I am the new owner of Wykeham Hall, the Duke of Carlisle. Please take my horse, rub him down good, and find him a stall and a meal." Jamie spied a younger lad peeking around the edge of the stables. "Come out, lad, and help your master..." Jamie raised an eyebrow at the stableman.

"Richards, milord,"

Jamie nodded with a smile. "Mr. Richards. And what is your name?" he asked the dirty blonde-haired boy. He was a young lad, just entering his teens, but he took Ajax's reins from Jamie and led him inside the barn.

"That's young Will, sir. He can't hear and don't talk well either. But he's a good boy, and Miss Eleanor has been teaching him his letters." Richards tugged nervously at his shirt sleeve as if afraid that Jamie would find fault with the arrangement.

"We didn't hear you were coming for a visit, milord." It was presumptuous for the servant to be questioning him, but Jamie had never stood on ceremony. If the man did his work well, Jamie would treat him fairly.

"I thought it time to inspect this property." Jamie nodded and turned to go back to the front entrance of the house, but stopped and turned back. "My coach will arrive soon, probably within an hour if they've had no issues."

"We'll take care of the horses when they get here, milord."

Jamie dipped his chin in acknowledgment. Then he headed toward the house. Once he arrived at the front door, he faced a dilemma. It was his house, so there was no reason he couldn't just walk right in, but he wasn't sure of the state of the staff, how many servants there were at Wykeham Hall. If there were no butler or footmen, he could stand outside for hours before someone discovered him and allowed him entrance.

On the other hand, the staff did not expect him, and it seemed wrong to just barge inside. In the end, he turned the doorknob and entered.

The hall was spacious, the floors set with marble. A massive table stood next to the door, and a gilded mirror hung over it, but it did not appear that any servants were around to greet him. A sweeping staircase came down from the upper floor, carpeted, with a beautifully carved mahogany rail. His cousin had at least spent coin to take care of the indoor living quarters. There must be a few servants because the hall was clean and maintained.

Jamie heard a sound and looked up to see a woman carefully stepping from stair to stair descending from the second floor. She had light brown hair pulled back in a neat bun and dressed in a black dress. She was maneuvering a cane with one hand and had a death grip on the railing with her other, so she didn't look up. Jamie couldn't tell how old she was, though the dress appeared too short by a few inches and it exposed a pair of trim ankles to view. He supposed she must be the housekeeper though he would need to increase her salary to ensure that she dressed the part. His cousin must have been paying too little if the woman wore such rags.

She stopped and closed her eyes, and her knuckles turned white on the railing. She was apparently in pain. Jamie dropped his hat and gloves on the table and was up the stairs in a few bounds. The woman opened her eyes, startled at his sudden appearance, and her body tilted. Jamie grabbed her just as she fell and swept her into his arms. She was a pleasant armful, he found, with luscious curves beneath the unflattering dress. The bodice was too tight, and she flailed, trying to cover herself with one hand while she waved the cane rather dangerously. She shrieked right in Jamie's ear, and he almost dropped her.

"Be still," he hissed while he adjusted the bundle in his arms. "I have you, but I will drop you if you keep moving like that."

"Unhand me at once!" She ceased her struggling, but she set her lips tight, and her face was white.

"Did you hurt yourself?" Jamie walked down the stairs.

"I... yes, my knee, but that was yesterday. I wrenched it again on the stair just now, but I'm all right. Please put me down, sir." They had reached the hall, and Jamie tightened his grip on her.

"Not until I find a suitable couch for you to rest on." He craned his head but wasn't sure which way to go, and the woman wasn't helping him. "If you injured your leg yesterday, you should not be up on it today. I'm sure the maids won't misbehave if you stay in your bed for another day."

"The maids? I don't..." she paused as he lifted her higher. He was a strong man, but he didn't want to stand there all day holding her, so he cleared his throat to remind her he had asked her a question of sorts. "Oh, that way. If you would take me to the library, I can sit in there with my leg up and read for a while. I'm not used to just sitting in my bed all day."

Jamie strode off in the direction she indicated. He turned and pushed a door open with his back, and he carried her into an extensive library and laid her on a sofa set in front of the empty fireplace. The woman reached for a blanket placed on the back and hastily spread it over her skirts.

Now she was settled, Jamie finally inspected her face. It shocked him. She was young, younger than himself by several years if he was any judge. And quite pretty. What kind of housekeeper did the old baron keep?

The woman was staring at him as well. Jamie shook off his thoughts as he bowed.

"May I get something more for your comfort? A book? A tea tray?"

"You may tell me who you are, sir, for I fear you have me at a loss."

"Many pardons, madame. I am your employer, the Duke of Carlisle."

Chapter Three

Eleanor blanched, and she pulled the blanket up to cover her too tight bodice. Mrs. Makepeace had borrowed Anna, the upstairs maid's second-best dress in the requisite black and left over from mourning her mother a year past. Anna was three inches shorter than Eleanor and not as endowed, but it was the best she could do until they could procure her clothes from the manse or find her something else to wear.

The Duke of Carlisle! What was he doing here? She felt her cheeks bloom with color as she took in the ramifications of his appearance. Eleanor peeked up from under her lashes to observe the man standing in front of her. He was tall with auburn hair and not exactly handsome, but still a good looking man. He was wearing riding apparel, but not a speck of mud spotted his shiny boots.

"My pardons, sir, um, Your Grace. I did not understand you were arriving."

"I did not send word ahead, Mrs.....?" He trailed off, and Eleanor realized that he was talking to her. Why did he assume her a married woman?

"Miss Mortimer," she replied and held out a hand that only shook just a little. "You must pardon my lack of a curtsey."

His eyes widened. "The Baron had an unmarried housekeeper? That is quite... unusual."

Eleanor's cheeks which had barely returned to normal burned even hotter as she realized what he meant. She withdrew her hand and placed it in her lap where she clenched both hands together until her knuckles turned white. Eleanor took a deep breath and gathered herself. She could explain to the Duke. After all, she had often had to deal with difficult parishioners for her father.

"Your Grace, I am not your housekeeper nor was I the late Baron's servant." Eleanor paused as his eyebrows went up, but he didn't speak though he clearly wanted to say *something*. "My late father was the rector of the local church. There was a... a..." she stammered, feeling foolish. "A tree fell on the manse two nights ago and damaged the building severely. Mrs. Makepeace, *your* housekeeper, insisted that I stay here at Wykeham Hall for the nonce until I can make other arrangements. Of course, I will expedite those arrangements now."

She attempted to stand, but His Grace motioned for her to stay. "Please, Miss Mortimer, do not attempt to rise. I take it that the injury to your..." he blushed and motioned to her legs. Eleanor was a country lass and of a practical nature, but apparently, Dukes did not mention extremities to young ladies. She watched fascinated as the color washed across his cheekbones before she recollected herself.

"I fell down the stairs when the tree came through the roof. I was fortunate that this was the only damage I sustained." Her body still ached, and Eleanor had bruises all over it, but she was not about to share that information with the Duke.

Mrs. Makepeace burst through the door, interrupting them. "Miss Eleanor, what are you doing out of bed?" She stopped dead as she saw the man standing in the library.

"Mrs. Makepeace. The Duke of Carlisle has arrived for a visit to Wykeham Hall. Your Grace, Mrs. Makepeace is the housekeeper here at Wykeham Hall and does a credible job at keeping the house immaculate." Eleanor found the accommodations luxurious which was a wonder as the old baron had been parsimonious and certainly the outside did not fare well.

Mrs. Makepeace curtsied, all in a flutter. She looked nervously at Eleanor, aware that they had overstepped boundaries in having her stay at the Hall. Eleanor heaved a sigh. The Duke caught the movement out of the corner of his eye but did not betray his thoughts.

"You've met Miss Eleanor then, Your Grace. A terrible time the lass has had, what with the tree collapsing the roof and the water damage from the rain. I thought, rather we thought it would be permissible for her to stay here, what with the house being mostly empty for now."

"But I will make other arrangements now," Eleanor cut in. "I cannot stay here with his Grace."

The Duke wrinkled his forehead. "Do you have other relatives in the area?"

"I was an only child, and my mother passed away some time ago. I do not know her family. My father has a brother, but he is in India, ministering to the natives."

A scowl appeared on the Duke's face, but whether he directed at her or her absent uncle, Eleanor did not know. "What about friends?"

Eleanor clenched her hands tight and lifted her chin. "Please do not worry, Your Grace. I will find my own accommodations."

He sliced a hand through the air, his eyes worried, but a small grin seemed to flit over his face. "That will not be necessary. My mother is on her way here. Meanwhile, Mrs. Makepeace may act as chaperone. Surely, we can make our way for a few days in this manner."

Eleanor protested, but he cut her off. "My dear Miss Mortimer, you have nowhere else to go at present. You are injured, you have just lost your father, and all your worldly possessions too, I suspect. The damage to your home is my responsibility, and so is your welfare. So, I shall hear no more about it."

Eleanor blinked back tears. In truth, she had nowhere to go. The village was not big and her choices meager.

The Duke turned back to Mrs. Makepeace. "I rode ahead, but my coach is behind me with my valet. I trust you can find quarters for us. Meanwhile, I will find a book for Miss Mortimer if you would be so good as to have a tea tray prepared. After that, I would like to meet with you to discuss the state of the household, the number of servants, and so forth unless there is a butler who I have not met yet."

Mrs. Makepeace shook her head vigorously. "Mr. Thorpe left after Baron Russell died and the agent never replaced him. However, Robert is our footman, and he can help you with anything you might need, Your Grace."

The Earl nodded a dismissal, and Mrs. Makepeace trotted out of the room. Eleanor thought she might run once she was out of sight, in a hurry to tell Cook and the other servants of the Duke's arrival.

The Duke cleared his throat. "Miss Mortimer, how many I serve you? What type of books do you like to read?"

"I've no idea what the Baron kept in his library, but as long as it's not an agricultural tract, I believe I can make do."

"A bluestocking?" the Duke blurted out, then blushed again. "Please pardon me. I did not mean that at all. I'm used to my mother reading in the same manner, and I tease her with that title. In my heart, I believe it a badge of honor. I prefer intelligent women."

A silence settled between them as Eleanor pondered his words. The Duke of Carlisle was not nearly as imposing as his appearance implied. She looked up as he moved to the shelves. The Baron seemed to have an extensive collection. Eleanor hoped that he had also amassed a variety of titles.

Without thinking, she called to the Duke. "Does your wife also read the books that your mother does?"

A book dropped to the floor with a slam, and Eleanor jumped. She could just see his back and watched as he bent over to pick up the book. He must ride regularly, she mused, as she admired the way his breeches tightened over his muscular legs.

Eleanor slapped her hands to her cheeks and lowered her face. How could she think like this of a married man? A man she had just met? She must have knocked her head in the fall down the stairs. Eleanor was mortified.

"I am not married." The Duke's voice was very deep as he replied to her original query, and Eleanor buried herself under the blanket with a moan. This was even worse, but it also explained his concern for a chaperone. The Duke was in a vulnerable position if anyone thought he had compromised her, ridiculous as the idea might be.

She heard footsteps, and the Duke appeared over the back of the sofa. "Are you all right? I thought there was a moan and supposed you might be in pain."

"I'm fine, Your Grace," Eleanor responded primly. She looked at the book in his hand. "Is that for me?"

His blue eyes crinkled in puzzlement as he parsed out her answer. "Yes." He handed her the tome.

"Waverly by Anonymous," Eleanor said as she opened the book. "I have not read this, but it looks new."

"It is actually by Walter Scott, about the Jacobite rebellion. It was very popular when it first came out a few years ago. My mother enjoyed it very much though I thought the first few chapters rather dry."

"You've read it?" Eleanor's mouth dropped open.

The Duke gave a dry chuckle. "Yes, Miss Mortimer, I read novels when I have the time. I agree with my mother in this; overall, the book was enjoyable."

He turned as Robert, the missing footman, stood in the door, a tray in his hands.

"Where would you like this, Miss Eleanor, um, Your Grace?" he stammered.

The Duke deferred to Eleanor. "On that table, if you please, Robert."

The Duke held up a hand, walked over and picked up the table, and brought it closer to the sofa where Eleanor lay. She struggled to rise, but again he held up a hand.

"Please remain where you are, Miss Mortimer. I believe I can serve us tea."

Eleanor marveled at the diverse aspect of a man who could convey orders with the lift of a hand while blushing at the mention of a woman's legs. She pushed more pillows behind her back as Robert set the tea tray on the table. The Duke dismissed the footman and then busied himself setting several cakes on a small plate. He passed the plate to Eleanor with a napkin and asked, "Miss Mortimer, how do you take your tea?"

"Just plain is sufficient, Your Grace."

He nodded and poured a cup, then handed it to her before he fixed his own repast. He dragged an armchair over to the table and dug into the food with gusto. Eleanor watched fascinated as he devoured several of the cakes between sips of tea. She realized how rude she was behaving when he looked at her over the brim of his cup, one auburn eyebrow raised in question.

She hastily applied herself to her own plate. Not that the Duke was rude about his eating as he was very fastidious. For whatever reason, in her own mind, Eleanor didn't imagine Duke's eating little pink cakes and sipping tea. She thought they'd rather swill down brandy with great haunches of venison on their plates. Perhaps she was thinking back to the time of Henry VIII. What did she actually know of Dukes? The Duke of Carlisle was the first one she had ever seen, much less talked to.

He sat back, only one cake left on the dish. "Would you like more tea? Or another cake?" he asked politely.

"Please, help yourself," Eleanor replied. He did not hesitate but promptly ate the last remaining pastry. Eleanor thought she would have to speak to Mrs. Makepeace about moving the dinner hour up. Tea would only satisfy the Duke for a short while.

"Do you need anything further, Miss Mortimer? I should try to meet the staff and find my way around the house." He rose as Eleanor shook her head.

"Thank you, Your Grace, but I believe I am perfectly happy here now. I have my book thanks to you, and I think I shall delve into Mr. Scott's story."

"Please call me when you are ready to retire back to your room, and I will help you upstairs. We would not want you to have any more accidents."

"Thank you, but I'm sure that won't be necessary. Robert can help me if I need it and I'm feeling much better. I can walk by myself just fine."

He gave her a stern look and shook his head. "If I must, I will make you promise. You must ask for aid. Else you could have permanent damage or at the least, be laid up for much longer."

Eleanor hesitated but finally nodded. She was independent and did not want to depend on another, but she was also practical and didn't want to be stuck in bed or on a sofa for any period of time.

She watched as the Duke crossed the room and walked out the door. Eleanor sighed. His arrival had complicated matters. Shaking her head, she opened her book and read the first page.

Chapter Four

After consulting with Mrs. Makepeace and meeting some of the rest of the staff, Jamie retired to the office where the old Baron kept the books for the estate. He pulled the most recent account book down and opened it on the massive desk. Then he explored the drawers and found paper and an ink pot.

Before he did anything else, Jamie needed to send a letter to his mother. He had told Miss Mortimer a small lie. His mother had no intention of coming to Devonshire, but he needed to get her here posthaste to act as a chaperone. Miss Mortimer was a lady of gentle birth despite not belonging to the nobility. It would not do for anyone to disparage her or her name. Nor did he want to be caught up in a forced marriage himself. If it weren't that he had determined that the estate needed to have time and work invested in it, Jamie would have been on Ajax riding back to London.

He started the letter explaining the situation he had found and asked for her help. Jamie knew it would delight his mother to come to his aid. She was devoted to her only child, not that she had ever spoiled him. Elizabeth Lennox was an Englishwoman, daughter of an Earl and the widow of a Duke. She made her way through society without a misstep, her charm and sweetness captivating one and all. Jamie took after his Scots father, more reserved and definitely shyer.

Jamie read over the letter after he had scribbled his name at the bottom. He paused as he reached the part where he inquired as to her success in finding a replacement for the late Reverend Mortimer, leaned back in his seat, and tapped the quill on his chin. What if the new vicar was also a single man in need of a wife?

He liked Miss Mortimer. Despite her troubles, she had a pleasant demeanor and a friendly humor. She showed bravery, Jamie thought, dealing with each obstacle as it came along with little of a fuss, at least in the short time he had known her. She was also pretty. Jamie swallowed hard as he thought about the full bosom that overflowed the too tight bodice. The display embarrassed her, but he understood she had lost her possessions and borrowed the gown. He had acted the gentleman, but it didn't stop him from sneaking a few peeks.

Jamie dipped the quill and added a postscript to the letter. His mother loved to act the matchmaker and if she could not find a wife for her son, perhaps seeking a spouse for the cleric would appease her.

THE NEXT DAY JAMIE rode out on Ajax to view the estate. He had spent an hour with Mr. Brown, his agent here at Wykeham Hall, looking at the books, and now the two were surveying the land and visiting the tenant farms. Jamie planned a stop at the village for lunch at the Highwayman Inn where he hoped to meet some of the locals.

By the time they reached the Inn, Jamie was ready to eat. He was a big man and liked his meals to be regular and filling. He retained no weight just like his father before him, so Jamie didn't see a problem with his consumption habits.

The proprietor of the Highwayman, a Mr. Rawlings, met them at the door. Word of his presence had spread through the area, and everyone knew who he was. His coach had driven through the village last evening on its arrival, alerting anyone not aware that the new owner of Wykeham Hall had arrived.

Only a few men were in the dining room at this time of day, but they turned and nodded at Jamie and Mr. Brown as they found seats. The meal was tasty, better than Jamie expected, a thick mutton stew and crispy brown bread hot from the oven. Even the ale was refreshing, not at all sour or thin as found in some inns in London.

His host attended on them but wasn't intrusive. Jamie and Mr. Brown could continue to discuss business as they ate. Jamie was careful in what he said, conscious of the ears in the room, but he asked questions, trying to learn more about the area and the people who lived here. It was when he enquired about the damaged manse that Mr. Rawlings popped over to their table, not even pretending he hadn't been eavesdropping.

"A terrible thing it was, Your Grace. Poor Miss Eleanor lying at the bottom of the stairs. I thought she was dead when I found her. Old Jed had passed by the house early and noticed the tree, so I went to check on her, her being all alone in the world."

This was an opportunity for Jamie to find out more about the erudite Miss Mortimer. The innkeeper obviously knew her well.

"It is fortunate that you were there to aid her in her time of strife. Does she have no family at all?"

"No, milord, not at all. The vicar has... had served this parish since Miss Eleanor was a baby. Her mother passed on when she was a wee lass, and she's grown up as her father's helpmate. Miss Eleanor is well-loved throughout the parish. She's the one that people come to with their troubles and needs, and the lass helps as best she can. She will be sore missed if she has to leave the village, but I don't know where she'd go. I imagine someone could hire her as a governess, but she deserves better than that." The innkeeper looked hopefully at Jamie, wanting Jamie to step in. Jamie could not divulge his own possible matchmaking plans for Miss Mortimer. Still, the thought of her as a governess, while she would be a good fit for that occupation, was distasteful to Jamie. Mr. Rawlings was correct that the lady deserved better than that resort.

"What of her possessions in the manse? Has there been an attempt to recover the lady's property?" Jamie thought he should change the subject from Miss Mortimer's virtues before someone realized that her actual virtue was in danger of being compromised. Not that anything physical would happen, he thought, growing warm at the thought. Just that she was staying in the house with him could compromise her in some people's eyes even with the housekeeper acting as chaperone. He hoped that his mother would make haste to Devonshire.

"No one has been inside since we helped Miss Eleanor and moved her up to Wykeham Hall. I 'spect the tree needs to cutting up and removing before it's safe to go upstairs. The tree fell right on her bedroom, and the rainwater destroyed what the tree didn't break. The manse needs a lot of work before a new vicar can move in." Mr. Rawlings shook his head and sighed. The other two men in the room nodded in agreement.

"Mr. Brown will make arrangements to have the tree removed. I intend to look inside the manse this afternoon and see if I can retrieve anything for Miss Mortimer. The lady direly needs clothing."

Every man in the room gaped at him in stupefaction, mouths dropping and eyes wide, as Jamie realized what he said. He sputtered, "I mean that her borrowed dress is ill-fitting, and she needs something more appropriate to wear." His face was bright red, and once more he cursed his fair Scottish complexion.

Mr. Rawlings looked at him suspiciously and said, "Worse comes to worst, the lass can find something to wear at a shop in Okehampton." Jamie tucked that thought away.

He rose, ready to move on. Jamie had a tremendous amount of work to do on this estate he had discovered. Whether he kept the property or sold it off, his conscience and training ensured that he would put it to rights. Jamie was too responsible not to fulfill a duty to the people under his care whether or not he had inherited the obligation. The old Baron had maintained the interior of Wykeham Hall well, but they had not kept up the exterior, outbuildings, and tenant farms for years. Jamie had looked at the books, and the accounting was not clear. Mr. Brown couldn't enlighten him, admitting that the income from the tenants was sufficient in his opinion, but the Baron had not permitted him to reciprocate with necessary repairs for the tenants. Jamie needed to spend much more time looking at the accounting.

Once outside, Jamie dismissed his agent. Jonathan Brown seemed capable, and he was more than ready to start on the tasks that Jamie had assigned him. Though the man didn't say so, Jamie suspected he had chafed at the previous lord's dictates. He mounted Ajax and slowly rode back toward Wykeham Hall, studying each building on the way. Today, more people were out, and he tipped his hat as he passed.

Once he reached the manse, Jamie dismounted and tied Ajax to a post out front. He ascended the steps and opened the door. No point in knocking. There were a long hallway and a narrow stairway to his right. Jamie looked at the stairs. It was a miracle that Miss Mortimer had not been more seriously injured in her fall. He started down the hall; the place smelled musty and damp, still permeated with water. A sitting room was on one side of the building and looked untouched; the vicar's study on the opposite side was the same. Jamie reached a closed door and attempted to open it. It only moved a few inches, jammed from the other side. He could see this was the kitchen, but couldn't open the door more. There was an ominous creaking, and he decided that it was unnecessary to go further.

Jamie backtracked and entered the study. The window had a broken glass that had allowed in water and the wind to blow papers and objects around the room, but it was not significant. He saw two silhouettes hanging on the wall, and he crossed the room to examine them closer. One was a young woman and the other a girl, the vicar's wife and daughter, he thought. Jamie carefully took them off the wall and wrapped them in his handkerchief, stowing them in his pocket. He thought Miss Mortimer would like to have these back.

A quick peek in the setting room assured him that there was nothing of a personal nature, at least as far as he could determine. He ascended the stairs, each wooden step creaking under his weight. The house was not big, unusual in his experience for a vicar's home. Any young man with a family wouldn't find it suitable, explaining, perhaps, why the Reverend Mr. Mortimer had stayed in the living so long. A room at the top of the stairs appeared to be the vicar's bedroom, neat and undisturbed. There was another small room used as a sewing room by Miss Mortimer. The door to her bedroom at the end of the hall hung from one hinge, a tree branch protruding. Mr. Rawlings was correct. Her room had sustained the most damage.

Jamie did not walk to her bedroom, not trusting the building supports. They would need to remove the tree before they could make any further examination.

A swathe of fabric caught his eye in the sewing room as he turned to leave. It was a dress, several years out-of-style, but dyed black recently. One sleeve was being hemmed, but perhaps he could retrieve it for Miss Mortimer until he could visit or send to Okehampton.

He bundled up the dress and headed back outside. Perhaps it would be better to raze the building and start new. The new vicar needed a place to stay, and once he arrived, he could find a room at Wykeham Hall for the time being. Jamie would have to speak to Mr. Brown about rebuilding the manse in its entirety.

Jamie stuffed the dress in a saddlebag and mounted Ajax. He patted his pocket, ensuring that Miss Mortimer's portraits were safe and then gave Ajax the signal to proceed. He had a lot of work to do.

Chapter Five

Eleanor slowly limped down the hallway. Today she had done away with the cane as the swelling in her knee was much reduced, and the pain gone unless she stepped wrong. She had spent the last two days in her bedroom to avoid the Duke of Carlisle, taking her meals on a tray and spending the rest of the time reading or worrying.

Today she was sick of being coddled. Mrs. Makepeace told her the Duke spent a great deal of time out on the estate and the rest of his time in his office. Eleanor thought it safe to venture out for a short walk in the gardens. Perhaps she would bring her book out and sit in the fresh air for a while.

She had finished Waverly and moved onto another Scott book, The Antiquary. The Baron must have enjoyed reading Walter Scott as his library seemed to contain several of his books. Eleanor enjoyed reading the story of the brave Highlanders and the thwarted romance of Edward and Flora. It was a disappointment when Edward settled for the more sedate Rose. Eleanor was secretly a romantic though she hid it in her secret self, far away from her practical exterior.

The black gown rustled around her ankles. Eleanor appreciated that the Duke had rescued the dress. It had belonged to her mother and fit much better than the one borrowed from Anna. She'd finished the slight alterations necessary while hiding in her bedroom, so that even if the storm had ruined the rest of her meager wardrobe, at least she had one proper dress for the time being. Eleanor was not vain and wore clothing appropriate for a vicar's daughter, but her recent experiences made her exceeding appreciative for what she had. She had lost almost all: her father, her clothes, and most of her possessions.

The Duke had also brought the portraits that hung in her father's study. Eleanor closed her eyes, holding back tears. It was very kind of the Duke to have regained those for her. Her father had treasured them, and so did Eleanor. The Duke's thoughtfulness was sweet and much appreciated. He could have left them behind, perhaps to be stolen or lost in the damaged building.

Still, the Duke was a major problem for her. Eleanor made her way into the library to rest her knee on her way outdoors. She sat on the sofa, the same sofa the Duke had placed her on his first day. Eleanor knew how it might look to the outside world for an unmarried lady to be staying in the same house as a single man. She would be compromised, and he forced to marry her if anyone knew. Yet, in her mind and she supposed many others, Eleanor was ineligible to be a Duchess.

Eleanor didn't know when the Dowager Duchess would arrive, but each day that passed increased the possibility of a scandal occurring. It didn't matter she had not seen the Duke since the afternoon of his arrival once he had assisted her back upstairs to her bedroom. Since then they had been busy with their own affairs. She had taken her meals on a tray in her bedroom, and Mrs. Makepeace said the Duke was eating on a tray in his office, absorbed in going over the estate's papers.

Eleanor knew the people in the village trusted her, but all it would take was one person to question the current arrangement, and it would force the Duke to marry her. She wondered he would take such a risk, but perhaps he thought his rank protected him. At any rate, she worried about her situation in the short term.

If she thought about the long-term, Eleanor would break down in tears. She had no home or personal possessions. She had saved a small amount of money, but it wouldn't last her long. Her best course would be to find a position as a governess as Eleanor liked children and had helped her father by teaching some of the smaller village children their letters. Her father educated her enough to perform the duties of a governess, but she knew no one nearby who had a position available. There was a family over towards Launceston, but Eleanor thought their children were grown enough that the boys were away to school. She would have to look in Exeter or Plymouth, one of the bigger towns or cities.

Perhaps the Duke knew of someone who needed help with their children. She should try to find him and ask him. Eleanor shifted on the sofa, uncomfortable at importuning him when he had already done so much to help her. On reflection, she thought it best to continue to avoid him, at least until his mother arrived. Maybe the Duchess would know of someone with an open position; that was more likely, the more she thought about it.

Eleanor picked up her book and pushed herself off the seat. She didn't want to think about her difficulties any longer. She would find a place to get lost in the words of Scott's book. What would happen would happen, and there wasn't much she could do about it at present. Eleanor cautiously tested her knee with one step, found that there was no pain, and hurried back out to the hallway.

She was not prepared to crash into a large male body as she came through the door. The smell of bergamot drifted in the air as two strong arms grabbed her and kept her from banging into the door frame.

"Miss Mortimer, I beg pardon. I did not see you there."

Eleanor reached up and tucked in a curl that had come loose in the collision. "Your Grace, it was my fault entirely. I did not look as I stepped out into the hall."

The Duke set her back, reassured that she would not fall, and dropped his arms. Now Eleanor could smell horse along with bergamot and realized that he must have just come in from outside. He spent most mornings riding the estate, either with Mr. Brown or alone, according to Mrs. Makepeace.

"You are walking without your cane?" His tone was so like that of her father that Eleanor felt her throat burn with repressed tears. He would often scold her in the same manner, worried that she wasn't taking care of herself.

"My knee is much better, Your Grace."

His forehead wrinkled, but he apparently decided that Eleanor knew best and let the subject drop.

"Are you reading Mr. Scott's book then?"

"I have finished Waverly and enjoyed it very much. I've moved on to his book *The Antiquary* now."

He nodded, then stood silent for a long moment and Eleanor felt awkwardness creeping in between them. She spoke at the same time as he and laughed nervously.

"Please, Miss Mortimer, go ahead. I did not mean to interrupt."

"I was just going to thank you again for your kindnesses. And I wondered if you had heard from your mother as to her arrival." Eleanor felt her nose go pink; it was a terrible habit she had when embarrassed.

"No, I expect she has only just received my letter," the Duke said with a friendly smile.

Eleanor blurted out, "Oh, I thought you told me she was on her way here." She watched, fascinated, as two spots of red appeared on the Duke's cheeks.

"Of course, I misspoke." He cleared his throat. "I'm not exactly sure when she will arrive."

Eleanor realized that he had lied to her. He must have sent for his mother once he understood the situation here. Who knew when the Duchess would arrive?

This was a disaster.

"Your Grace, I wonder if you've received any newspapers since you arrived?" Eleanor asked.

"I have one I brought from London. If you don't mind that the news is weeks old, then yes, I have a newspaper." The Duke looked quizzical but was too polite to ask what she wanted it for. Ladies might read the gossip columns, but Eleanor was not the kind of woman who cared what was going on in the Ton. He would determine that within two minutes of meeting her.

"May I borrow it?"

"Of course, it is in my office. This way," he said, and he held an arm out to let her go first. Eleanor preceded the Duke, aware of him following her. She couldn't remember the time she had associated with a man as... viral, she supposed, as the Duke. He was a big healthy male, titled and wealthy. Why wasn't he married, she wondered?

She stepped into the room the Baron had used for an office. Papers and account books covered the big desk, messy in a way that Eleanor didn't associate with the fastidious Duke. He walked around her to the desk and moved piles of paper, looking for the promised newspaper.

Eleanor moved to the desk to help. Scribbled notes with smudged ink were everywhere. She could barely read the writing. This could not be the Duke's work — could it?

The Duke looked up, and Eleanor schooled her face, but she was too late. He must have caught the confused look as she surveyed the desk. The red spots on his fair skin which had faded flared once more. A wry smile lit his face, and Eleanor abruptly felt his charm.

"I see you're amused by my work habits." He waved a hand over the desktop.

Eleanor shook her head. "No, no, Your Grace. Indeed, I am not."

He held up a hand, and Eleanor ceased speaking. "You do not offend me, Miss Mortimer. My handwriting has long been the despair of my factors. Despite my tutors' best efforts, I am maladroit. I use my left hand for most activities and never adapted otherwise."

Eleanor felt an instant sympathy. Her father was left-handed also, and she had learned to write out his letters and sermons to improve the legibility of his missives.

"Your Grace," she began, but he interrupted.

"Miss Mortimer, is it possible for you to call me Carlisle? I am not so formal I want to be Your Grace'd by my acquaintances. That is what my intimates call me, or Jamie when we are private."

Eleanor considered. He was the first person of such rank she had ever met. It would be daring on her part to call him by his first name, but she couldn't see they would have much opportunity to be private together.

"Your Grace, I will do so on one condition — rather two." She added a finger to the one she was holding up. At his nod, she continued, "You must call me Eleanor, and you must allow me to aid you with your paperwork. My father also used his left hand primarily, and I assisted him with his papers. My handwriting is good, and I could act as your secretary if you'd like."

Eleanor folded her hands together in front of her and waited. The Duke glanced at the open door, his lips pursed as he thought, then back down to his messy desk.

"Miss Mortimer, Eleanor, I would be pleased to accept your offer if you are sure that is what you want. As you can see, I desperately need the help."

"Your Grace, it pleases me to return the favor even if it is not nearly equal to the aid you have rendered me. Please consider me as your secretary for the future."

"I confess, I did not think I would live here for the time it appears I will be staying. I left my secretary in London to take care of my other business and estates, thinking I could handle the work needed here, but I've found that there is much more to be done than I expected."

Eleanor placed her novel down on a nearby table and pulled a chair up to the other side of the desk. "Then let me begin, Your Grace."

"Jamie."

Eleanor looked up with a small smile. "Jamie," she said.

Chapter Six

Jamie tried very hard to ignore Eleanor over the next few days, but it was difficult. He cleared an area on a corner of the desk for her to work on, and she set to copying documents almost immediately. She worked industriously, her penmanship neat and legible. Occasionally, Eleanor asked him a question about a word he had smudged worse than others, but it amazed him at how well Eleanor could interpret his writing. She told him her father was much the same, but she did better at transcribing than his secretary in London ever had.

He found that he enjoyed her company. Eleanor did not indulge in idle chatter but responded when he asked a question. She knew everyone in the area and could add considerably to his knowledge of his tenants and the other local notables. So far, Jamie had not had company, but he expected that to change as time passed and people spread the news of his continued residence at Wykeham Hall throughout the countryside. Most had probably expected him to make a flying visit, as had Jamie himself, but he found that he didn't mind the delay. He was enjoying himself.

Wykeham Hall was a charming home. Less and less he thought he would sell the estate. The books were still undecipherable, but Jamie sensed the property could prove profitable if managed well. It was his duty to take care of the people attached to the estate.

Foremost among those was Miss Mortimer. Work had begun on the manse, the tree removed, and they had retrieved more of her possessions. Most of the interior at the back of the house was a total loss. Jamie had given orders that the rebuilding would expand the manse. There was enough room now that the tree was out of the way.

Jamie realized he had stopped writing and was staring at Eleanor only when she looked up and caught him. She lifted an eyebrow in a perfect arc, and he shrugged and went back to his papers. Thinking about the manse brought Eleanor to mind. Not only had it been her home for many years, but if his matchmaking plans bore fruit, it would be her future home. The expansion he planned to add could house her future children.

A blot of ink splashed on the letter to his factor at Dalemain, his prime estate in Cumbria. Jamie hastily blotted the paper, but he had pretty much destroyed it. He looked up at Eleanor to see if she has spied his mess, but she was discreetly ignoring it. The faint blush on her cheeks convinced him it was just a pretense.

Miss Mortimer would be a good mother, Jamie thought. A frisson of distaste passed through him at the thought, and Jamie bent his head down, disturbed. Why would he care if Eleanor married the new vicar and they had children together to rear in the manse? After all, that was his plan, to find an eligible single man to fill the vacancy at the vicarage and in Eleanor's life.

Disturbed at the direction of his thoughts, Jamie pushed away from the desk. "Miss Mortimer, I think I would like to go for a walk and clear my head. The paperwork grows tedious."

"Yes, Your Grace. I will continue here just a little longer as I'd like to finish this letter."

"I was asking if you'd like to accompany me, Eleanor. The letter can wait, and you have been toiling away industriously for days without respite." Eleanor's cheeks bloomed with color most attractively as she protested, but Jamie held up a hand to stop her. "I get outside most mornings on my ride, but you have not strayed from the house to my knowledge."

"Your Grace," Eleanor rolled her eyes as Jamie tilted his head, "sorry, Jamie, I am perfectly fine here. I go for a walk most mornings around the estate while you are on your ride, so there is no need for me to interrupt my tasks at this point."

Perversely, Jamie determined that Eleanor accompany him on his walk. He had discovered a stubborn streak in her, but Jamie was half-Scots and headstrong himself. He could also be devious.

"I would like you to come with me, Eleanor, as I hoped that you could give me a tour of the gardens. I have not yet inspected them and today is pleasant weather."

Eleanor rose and shook out her skirts. Jamie had noticed that she was a dutiful woman despite her occasional stubbornness. Eleanor had spirit, but she liked to be useful, sometimes to the extreme. It was an admirable quality for a vicar's wife, he thought. For any man's wife.

She took his arm once they were outside, and he led her around the corner of the house to where some flower beds were laid out. They weren't very expansive and sorely needed maintenance. It was another place where the Baron had inexplicably cut costs.

Eleanor mirrored his thoughts. "I have done a bit of gardening in the mornings, but the grounds need a keeper. The Baron let Mr. Langton go a few years ago, and the gardens have run wild."

"Langton was the groundskeeper?" Jamie asked. At Eleanor's nod, he inquired further, "Is he still in the area?"

"Mr. Langton retired and lives just outside Sourton. His son also trained in that work, but has taken up sheep farming as he could not find the work he preferred locally."

"I should speak to him and see if it interests him in taking over the grounds here." Jamie paused as Eleanor stopped to examine a rose in full bloom. She bent down to sniff at the flower which contrasted prettily against her black dress. Jamie pulled out a penknife and cut the stem, then trimmed away the thorns.

He handed her the flower. "With my compliments."

Eleanor smiled and curtsied. "My thanks, Your Grace."

Jamie grinned back. Eleanor had a lovely smile.

They turned to continue their walk, Eleanor on his arm as she held the rose to her nose. "There is a herb garden in the back near the kitchen garden. Cook has maintained those." She blinked as she lifted her head, looking at the sun. "I should have worn a hat — if I had a hat to wear. I could have borrowed one from Anna or Mrs. Makepeace, I suppose."

"That reminds me. I was planning an expedition to Okehampton tomorrow. I thought you might like to accompany me and do shopping to replace some of the personal items destroyed by the storm."

"That would be wonderful," Eleanor said. "I would appreciate that very much."

At that moment, Robert came running around the corner of the house. He slowed when he saw them, but headed straight to where they walked. Jamie paused, waiting to hear what Robert wanted.

"Your Grace, you have visitors. Mrs. Beaton and Miss Beaton are waiting in the sitting room. Shall I tell them you're available?"

The sitting-room windows looked out toward the gardens so Jamie couldn't see how he would be unavailable. Mrs. Beaton and her daughter had probably been spying on them.

"No, we will be in momentarily. Would you have Cook send a tea tray?" Robert nodded and returned the way he had come.

Eleanor looked stricken. "Perhaps you should go, and I will enter through the kitchen and go back to copying my letter," she suggested hesitantly.

"Eleanor, you would not desert me now. I know nothing about Mrs. Beaton or her daughter," Jamie teased.

"Your Grace, it is not seemly," Eleanor bit her lip and stared at the house. "they should not see me with you. Some might take it wrong."

"You mean Mrs. Beaton, I suppose." Perhaps it was reckless, but at that moment, Jamie didn't care. Why should Eleanor skulk in the back door because of some woman who took an inopportune time to pay a visit? Then common sense reasserted itself, and he reluctantly agreed. "Perhaps that's for the best."

Eleanor nodded and set off for the back of the house. With any luck, the Beatons would think she had just come out to give him a message. Jamie squared his shoulders and headed inside to meet his visitors.

Mrs. Beaton was a tall, thin woman with a great beak of a nose. Her daughter had most fortunately inherited her nose from her father, it seemed, but her figure from her mother. They were sitting when Jamie walked into the room, and he breathed a sigh of relief. Perhaps they had not viewed him walking in the gardens with Eleanor.

"Your Grace, welcome to Devonshire. We are so pleased to make your acquaintance." The lady held out a hand, and Jamie made the proper bows. Robert brought the tea tray in at that moment, and there was a bustle as Mrs. Beaton took over the serving.

"What a shame you don't have a lady here to do the honors, Your Grace," Miss Beaton observed and batted her eyes at him. Her mother beamed, but Jamie had all he could do not to make a tart remark.

"Indeed, I expect the Dowager Duchess any moment, and she will assume hostessing duties. I did not expect to be staying so long here, but I find the estate needs work, and I am quite enjoying my stay."

"I would imagine that you will receive a number of visitors, Your Grace. The company is thin here in this part of the country, and people like to be social."

Jamie nodded in agreement, but the truth was that he did not especially like being sociable. He enjoyed people, but he also liked his privacy. The endless social rounds in London bored him to tears as it had Lucy. It was one reason he thought he and Lucy would suit as husband and wife; she hated the social rounds. Funny he had not thought about Lucy in days. Jamie hoped that she had resolved her differences with de Vere. Perhaps she was happily married by now.

He realized that Mrs. Beaton had asked him a question while his thoughts had meandered. "I beg pardon, I didn't quite hear that."

"Your Grace, we wondered if you planned any entertainments during your stay. Perhaps after your mother arrives?"

Miss Beaton added, "One is so starved for company here." She batted her eyes again and showed her teeth, giving her a startling resemblance to his horse, Ajax.

It was most unfortunate.

"Perhaps," he responded. "I will consult with my mother when she arrives."

Mrs. Beaton nodded, satisfied with his answer, and they continued to converse about the local people and happenings. For someone who indicated that there wasn't much of a society here, Mrs. Beaton seemed to have an active social life.

Miss Beaton caught Jamie's attention when she inquired about the new vicar. "We cannot wait to meet him. We miss Reverend Mortimer, of course. It is so sorrowful for Miss Mortimer. First, her father and then her home destroyed. But you have made great strides in restoring the manse. We saw the work as our carriage came through the village."

"Yes, I hope that my mother will bring the new vicar with her when she arrives. He will need to stay here until they complete the work on the manse."

"Can you tell us something about him?" Miss Beaton inquired, a glint in her eye.

"Sad to say, I cannot. I left finding a replacement in my mother's capable hands, and I'm sure he will perform his duties admirably."

Miss Beaton sat back, disappointment clear on her face. Either she wanted gossip to pass on, or she had hopes for the man. She would suffer a disappointment if Jamie had his way about matching him with Eleanor.

"They shall miss Miss Mortimer in the village, I daresay. She was very well liked. We stopped and inquired of Mr. Rawlings where she might have gone, but he couldn't say. I suppose she has taken a position as a governess or some such." Mrs. Beaton put her teacup down in what Jamie could only hope was a prelude to her departure. He made a mental note to thank Rawlings for his forbearance in passing on any news about Eleanor.

Mrs. Beaton stood, followed by her daughter who hastily stuffed the last bit of scone in her mouth, and Jamie followed them out to their carriage. He bade them goodbye with some relief and returned to his paperwork in the office. And to Eleanor whose serenity was welcome after the Beatons' visit.

The red rose sat in a glass in the corner of his desk, near to where Eleanor was bent over writing.

Chapter Seven

The curricle sped along at a good pace. Eleanor had only ridden in a similar coach once before, but she enjoyed the open view as they passed along. The vehicle had belonged to the Baron as well as the horses pulling it, but Jamie had decided it would do for their trip into Okehampton. Eleanor was sitting next to him, sometimes too close as ruts in the road bounced her nearer until she inched away again. He took up a lot of the seat, so that wasn't always easy, but the only other vehicle they could have used was his traveling coach, and that was too big.

The other option was riding, but Eleanor was an uncertain rider, not having ridden much. Her father had a pony and cart he allowed Eleanor to use when she needed it. Jamie was appalled though he tried to hide it and promised that he would provide riding lessons for her as soon as possible so she could go out riding with him and practice. Eleanor wondered at his insistence. There was no need for her to exercise her riding skills. Governesses did not ride horses.

During the last few days, she found the missing newspaper, and Jamie had received several others in the mail. There were a few promising advertisements, and she had replied to three. They were all far away from Devonshire, but Eleanor knew the old saw about beggars and choosers. She had asked Jamie to frank the letters but hadn't told him what they were for, and he was too polite to ask. He added them to the pile of outgoing messages of his own.

Eleanor enjoyed working with Jamie on his correspondence. She wanted to be useful, to make up for him letting her stay at Wykeham

Hall. Besides, she didn't like to be idle all day. She wasn't used to it and didn't much care for it. Eleanor had often performed the same tasks for her father, and a Duke's communications were so much more interesting.

Jamie's interests ranged far and wide to a woman who had spent most of her life in one small area of the country. He had estates all over England and Scotland, also one in Ireland. He was obviously wealthy, but also worked hard at the responsibility of his position. Eleanor wondered that he was remaining at Wykeham Hall for so long. There was no reason he couldn't delegate the tasks of the estate to Mr. Brown and be on his way back to London. Maybe he would leave once his mother arrived.

"You should buy a riding habit if you can find one," Jamie broke into her thoughts.

Eleanor laughed. "I don't think so. My accounts cannot afford a garment I would only wear once or twice. I must be practical."

"I plan to cover your expenses on this trip, Eleanor. I owe you recompense for your scribing and other help."

"Your Grace, I cannot allow that" Eleanor was distraught. She didn't have much in the way of savings, but she had a small inheritance from her mother that would cover the few things she intended to buy. That would have to do until she received income as a governess, but it would not stretch to frivolities.

"We'll see," was his only rejoinder.

Eleanor didn't reply, but she would not allow the Duke to pay for her clothing. She was already living under his roof, and it would not do to have him contribute any further to her situation. Gentlemen did not buy clothing for ladies. Eleanor may not have been in society much, but she knew that. Reading widely had its advantages.

They spent much of the trip with Eleanor pointing out some of the sights along the way, and Jamie contrasting Devonshire with other parts of England and Scotland. His descriptions of the Highlands fascinated Eleanor. They sounded beautiful, stark but majestic. Maybe someday she would visit them.

They reached the outskirts of Okehampton, and Jamie found a place to board the horses while they did their shopping and other errands. The first place they headed was a dressmaker's shop. In London, the shop would have been under a French name, but here the sign only said 'Dressmaker.'

A buxom woman with a head of blonde curls greeted them, eying them curiously. Before Jamie could take over, Eleanor stepped forward and explained her needs.

Mrs. Glass, the proprietress, assured Eleanor that she could help her though it might take a few days to assemble all she needed. She had one dress in a gray color she thought she could alter to fit Eleanor almost at once and another in black that just required hemming. She would just have her assistant take Eleanor's measurements if she stepped behind the curtains. Eleanor complied, and the assistant commenced with her tape and writing numbers down.

Eleanor could hear Jamie speaking with Mrs. Glass, but their tones were indistinguishable. She hoped he was just passing pleasantries, but Eleanor suspected his motives. He seemed determined to help her despite her protests.

Mrs. Glass promised to have the black dress ready for her to pick up before they left town. Eleanor thanked her and promised to pay when she returned for the gown, but Mrs. Glass insisted that she would send a bill to her at Wykeham Hall.

"Miss, that is our usual practice. I assure you that the amount will be as we have decided. But I like to be sure you wear the gown at least once, and the workmanship satisfies you."

Until now, Eleanor had made all her own gowns, and she was unsure enough of the selling practices of a dressmaker she acquiesced. She suspected that Jamie had made arrangements with Mrs. Glass while she was being measured, but she vowed that if the bills were not what she expected, then she would settle it with him at once.

After the dressmaker visit, they strolled to an apothecary's store. Jamie left Eleanor there to do shopping for personal items while he went on to the bank. They agreed to meet at a bookseller in an hour. Eleanor made her purchases and then proceeded to the bookstore. A new novel by Miss Austen about a naval captain and a young woman engrossed her.

Eleanor enjoyed the other books by this author, and this new book tempted her to buy it, but she worried about the expenditures she had already made that day. She needed to be careful with her budget, and this was an unwarranted expense. She was putting the book back on the shelf with some regrets when Jamie came up behind her.

"What is this? A new book by Miss Austen!" Jamie reached past her and pulled the book back out.

"You know Miss Austen? Oh, I suppose you do. Her books are so popular." Eleanor smiled at Jamie. She couldn't help it, his excitement was contagious.

"I'll have you know I have read all her books and have the bound set in the library at Carlisle House. It was very sad when she passed away."

"Yes, this one was published after her death," Eleanor replied.

"I must have it. Perhaps you could read it to me in the evenings?"

Eleanor almost dropped her reticle in surprise. They had begun to dine together, at first trays in the office, but then Mrs. Makepeace insisted that they eat together in the dining room. The housekeeper had a matronly manner that Jamie didn't seem to mind even if he was a Duke. Though he was the least 'Dukish' person she had ever met. Still, they parted after dinner, Eleanor back to her chambers and Jamie to the library or his office. They didn't spend their evenings together.

"I suppose that would be nice," she answered slowly. Jamie was a kind man, but it must bore him, so long here in the country. She wouldn't be here herself much longer once she got a response from one of her governess queries. So what harm could it do to spend the evening reading together?

Jamie browsed the shelves while Eleanor watched, envious of the pile of books he so freely selected. If she ever had the money, she would buy books over dresses, but Jamie was a wealthy man and could afford whatever he wished. She saw how hard he worked and knew he deserved his rewards, such as they were. Eleanor would not begrudge him his stack of books, but she admired a man who would value his reading more than a new frock coat.

He completed his purchases, taking two volumes including the Austen with them and having the rest sent to the estate. Then Jamie took her to a local inn for luncheon. This was a great treat for Eleanor. She seldom ate a meal in public, and the variety of people at the inn fascinated. Again, Jamie fit right in, not making an issue or asking for special treatment because of his status. Rather, he was friendly with the people around him and enjoyed his meal while including Eleanor in conversation and seeing to her comfort in this different environment.

After they had stopped once more at the dressmaker's to retrieve her gown, Eleanor and Jamie proceeded to where they had left the horses and carriage. Rounding a corner, they almost collided with Mrs. Beaton and her daughter. Eleanor wanted to turn and walk the other way when Mrs. Beaton's eyes widened in shock, and Miss Beaton let out an audible gasp. Jamie did not release her arm, but bade the ladies a pleasant "good afternoon." Still, Eleanor could feel the tension in his arm.

"Your Grace, Miss Mortimer, how unexpected to see you here — together." Mrs. Beaton pursed her lips, and Miss Beaton tittered behind a gloved hand.

"We did not expect to see you again so soon," Jamie replied enigmatically.

"Miss Mortimer, we were so sad to hear of your recent misfortunes. As I said to the Duke yesterday, we had no idea where you had gone. I didn't know you knew people in Okehampton."

Eleanor forced a smile, knowing Mrs. Beaton would make trouble. She replied, but Jamie answered first.

"I was pleased to run into Miss Mortimer here and happy to see her situation so improved."

Mrs. Beaton narrowed her eyes, suspicious of Jamie's intervention, but Eleanor grasped the straw he had tossed. "The Duke was very helpful to me after the destruction of my home." There, neither of them had actually lied, just evaded any truths. "But I must apologize, I have errands to run so I will leave you now."

Jamie bowed, but let her walk off. Eleanor's heart was pounding, and she hoped that the Beaton women would not question him further. Jamie understood the stakes here. If the Beaton's started any gossip about them, it would force them to marry.

Eleanor was acknowledging that she was not so averse to a forced marriage any longer. Jamie was an attractive man, not only in looks but in manner. Yet no matter how marriage to him might solve her difficulties, it would not be fair to him. He needed to marry someone of his rank. Eleanor was a gentlewoman, but she could not claim more than that. It was best that the Beatons believe theirs had been a chance meeting.

She walked around a corner and waited, fidgeting with her packages as she marked the time until Jamie caught up with her. A moment later, he strode down the street, a scowl on his face. Eleanor grimaced, but he shook his head and took her arm.

"It's time we left Okehampton," he said, and they hurried to the stables. Though she was dying to know what was said, Eleanor didn't speak until the horses were well outside of town headed back to Sourton.

"What else did you say to Mrs. Beaton?" It was a bit blunt, but Eleanor had been stewing for a while.

"We chatted about a possible dinner engagement at her home once my mother arrives," Jamie replied, his eyes narrowed as he glanced at Eleanor.

"That's all? She didn't ask about me anymore?"

"No, once you were on your way, she appeared to dismiss you from her mind."

Eleanor slumped back in relief. Perhaps they had been lucky.

That's when she made the mistake of saying so to Jamie.

Chapter Eight

Jamie gritted his teeth. "Are you so set against marriage or is it only to me?"

Eleanor edged away from him as far as she could on the narrow seat. "What?"

Jamie swallowed and moderated his tone. "Is it only me you would not wish to marry or are you against the institution in general?"

Eleanor sat up straight, wrinkled her nose, and pursed her lips. Jamie did not lose his temper often, but he was dangerously close now. The encounter with the Beaton's and Eleanor's reaction had set him off. He wasn't even sure why. He'd have to examine that feeling closer once they reached Wykeham Hall.

"Your Grace, I am terribly sorry..."

"Do not call me Your Grace!" Jamie thundered. Then he grabbed Eleanor's arm as she backed up more and nearly fell out of the curricle. With the other hand, he pulled the horses to a stop in the middle of the road. Eleanor stared at him, white-faced and trembling, and abruptly Jamie felt terrible.

"Eleanor, Miss Mortimer, I am deeply ashamed of my behavior. I beg your pardon, and I hope you can forgive me my intemperate conduct." Jamie released Eleanor's arm, and she shakily drew in a breath. Her face was a mask as she reseated herself and faced forward.

"I am not against the institution of marriage, Your Grace," she intoned. "I remember my mother, and my parents' happiness together. But I *do* feel that marriage to you, a forced marriage would be a terrible mistake."

Jamie drew in a deep breath, but he remained silent, willing her to continue. He knew why it would be a mistake — people of the Ton married for status or wealth, business alliances of a sort. But he wanted to hear why *she* thought it would be wrong.

Eleanor looked at him out of the corner of her eye and sighed. "Your station is high above me. You need to marry someone of your own class. And I intend to be a governess so marrying anyone at this point is impossible."

"Governess? Is that what those letters were about?"

"Yes, Your Grace. I can't reside at Wykeham Hall much longer. The incident with the Beaton's assures me of that. While I would let my reputation be tarnished if I must to save yours, I'd rather that didn't happen."

"Yes, I see," Jamie wasn't sure he saw, but he would let it go for now. He flicked the reins to set the horses in motion. "But Eleanor, call me Jamie, please. I think we are friends and friends may be informal."

"Of course." She ventured a small smile. "Are we friends, Jamie?"

"Yes," he replied firmly.

They drove along for a way before Jamie spoke again.

"I was to marry once."

Startled, Eleanor looked around at him, but he kept his eyes on the horses.

"Actually, I asked a lady to marry me recently. We are friends, and I thought could make a good match, but she is in love with someone else." His lip tipped up in a little smile. "With any luck, he married Lucy already."

Eleanor stayed silent, but Jamie could tell she was listening.

"But the time I speak of was when I was much younger, barely out of university. She was a few years older than me, the daughter of an Earl, and I was madly in love with her. Now I know that it was just infatuation, but at the time..." he trailed off and clucked at the horses to pick up the pace.

"What happened?" Eleanor asked.

"She married someone else. She was just toying with me. I am a Duke, and she wanted the title. But my Scots blood was enough to have her turn to another eligible Duke when she had the chance. He was much older, but she is a Dowager Duchess now with a small son who inherited the title, so she got somewhat what she wanted."

"Why would anyone care if you are part Scots?" Eleanor was sputtering in indignation, and Jamie laughed. Her ire eased a hurt in his heart he didn't even know he still carried.

"To the Ton, anyone who is not pure English carries a stigma. At least, I'm not part French," and he pretended to shiver in horror. Eleanor leaned against him for a second just to show her sympathy, Jamie suspected. To his alarm, the contact caused a reaction in a different part of his body. He caught a whiff of her lavender scent and got harder. The tips of his ears caught fire as he tried to think how to relieve his plight. He tried to tug his jacket over the protuberance without attracting Eleanor's attention.

It didn't work. She said nothing, but he knew she had seen. Eleanor may be a vicar's daughter, but she was also a country lass. She turned her head to look out at the passing countryside, but her cheeks were a rosy red.

Neither said anything for the rest of the way home.

ELEANOR CAME TO DINNER in her new gown. Jamie wished that she could wear a pastel muslin that would suit her coloring more, but the black dress was a vast improvement over the refurbished one she had previously worn and much better than Anna's borrowed frock.

They sat together at one end of the long table in the dining room. Jamie could have sat in the breakfast room which was much cozier, but he suspected that Mrs. Makepeace enjoyed the pomp of using the formal dining area. He enjoyed his evening meals there with Eleanor.

She was so well-read that conversation never lagged. Jamie's night dragged once she left the table, so it pleased him that he had hit on the idea of her reading to him after their meal.

He eagerly joined her in the sitting room after their meal, his new book in hand. Jamie tired of the paperwork for the estate, the endless lists, and letters he needed to do to put the property back to his satisfaction. Jamie pushed aside the niggling thought said he should delegate this work and attend to his affairs back in London. Nothing was pressing in the city, and he was enjoying his sojourn in the country.

And his time with the vicar's daughter.

Eleanor smiled as he passed her the Austen novel and bowed. Jamie took a seat in the chair opposite her and watched as she opened the book and read. Miss Austen wrote well, and her latest story was interesting. It was about two former lovers who had separated because the woman thought the man not good enough for her. Now their fortunes were reversed when they met again several years later.

Eleanor had a good voice for reading aloud. She kept a steady pace with just enough inflection to hold one's attention to the story. Not that the book didn't keep Jamie's attention — it did, but he found himself distracted by the expressions on her face as she read, the way her hand gracefully turned the pages, or her eyes as she occasionally glanced up at him.

This was not good.

Jamie meant Eleanor for the new vicar, whoever he might be. The man had better be worthy of her. If he were not, then Jamie would ensure that Eleanor had other options. Governess! An attractive woman like Eleanor should not work as a governess. Supposed she ended up in the household of a lecher who pursued her against her will. It could ruin her. Why should she have to care for another woman's children, anyway? She should marry happily, and the children should be her own.

That was when Jamie realized that he was falling in love with Eleanor. He had thought he'd been in love with Lydia years before, but that was an infatuation. He admired and like Lucy, but that was friendship.

With Eleanor, it was more. Certainly, she attracted him physically — the episode in the carriage today assured him of that fact, and her also to his mortification. He admired her strength and smiled at her stubbornness. Jamie liked everything about her. She might not realize it, but she would make a perfect Duchess.

He must have made a noise because Eleanor paused and looked up. "Is something the matter?"

"No, no, everything is fine. I beg your pardon. I did not mean to interrupt. Just a sudden thought triggered by the story," he responded.

Eleanor looked down at the book with a puzzled look but continued to read. In fact, Jamie did not misspeak. In some regards, the story of the book followed this thought. Eleanor did not want him forced to marry her because she thought her rank was inferior. Jamie wondered how she'd feel if it wasn't a prescribed arrangement because of a perceived scandal. He *felt* she liked him but was wary of his rank. Could it be more and did she have feelings for him also?

"Did you fall asleep?" Eleanor's amused voice distracted him from his thoughts.

Jamie looked up, startled at the interruption and blushed. "No, not at all. Your voice is soothing."

Eleanor laughed, "And can put one to sleep. My father used to say the same." She sobered as she placed the book on a nearby table, and Jamie frowned. Not much time had passed since the death of her father. She reminded him daily of how close they were.

He rose from his chair and walked over to Eleanor. Her eyes widened as he loomed over her, but he reached out a hand to her. She placed her hand in his, her brow wrinkled in uncertainty. Jamie pulled her up and into his arms.

"I think you need a hug," he said. She was stiff in his arms, but gradually relaxed and placed her head on his chest. Jamie did no more than hold her for a minute, then released her and stepped back.

"Eleanor, I am sorry for your loss. I know how much you miss your father."

She blinked away tears until Jamie handed her his handkerchief, then carefully wiped her cheeks.

"Thank you," she said as she handed the cloth back to him. "You're right. I miss my father very much. He's all I had in the world." Eleanor attempted a smile, but it was weak, and her chin trembled.

"I hope you know I am here for you also, Eleanor."

She shrugged and turned away. Jamie cursed under his breath and then reached for her arm and turned her back to face him.

"Eleanor, I mean it. I'll do whatever I can to help you." Her eyes widened at the intensity of his speech, but Jamie needed to make her understand. "You will never want as long as I can see to your needs."

"Thank you, but it is unnecessary. I'm not your responsibility, Your Grace, though I appreciate your many kindnesses."

He sighed. "Jamie. Eleanor, call me Jamie."

She rolled her eyes. "I find it hard to do so when you are making pronouncements in your ducal tone."

"Ducal tone?" A grin quirked up the corner of his mouth, and his eyes lit up in laughter.

"You know what I mean," she huffed. "You order me about. It's disconcerting then to address you familiarly after that. I feel I should polish your boots instead."

Jamie laughed, a deep belly laugh, and Eleanor joined in. When the guffaws faded away, Jamie realized that Eleanor was only standing a step away. He could pull her into his arms and taste her lips, the lips that had been keeping him awake at night. Eleanor looked like she wanted him to, her eyes still shining and her lips plump and moist.

It was one of the hardest things he had ever done, to step away from her, but he did not want to take a chance they would be forced into marriage by being caught in a compromising situation. The servants had not balked at their proximity so far, probably because they trusted Miss Eleanor and knew she had no other recourse. Mrs. Makepeace, Richard, and the maids all kept a close eye on them. The door to the office was always open when they were working together, and it amazed Jamie at how often one of the servants seemed to pass by. He respected their concern, but his whole body rebelled as he moved away.

Eleanor looked down and said in a low voice, "It is late and time, I think, to retire."

Jamie nodded solemnly and watched as she walked out of the room. Then he headed for the decanter sitting on a shelf on the opposite wall.

Tonight might be a good time to get raging drunk.

Chapter Nine

Eleanor was busy copying out a list of improvements needed for the tenant farms on the estate at Wykeham Hall. Jamie continued to pore through the account books. Mathematics was not her strong point, but even Eleanor could tell that there were discrepancies in the accounts. The estate had a healthy income, but the money wasn't dispersed back out where needed. Yet, it was also not to found. Eleanor knew the Baron was not a gambler as he never left the estate, but what else he could have done with the money she didn't know and couldn't guess.

Jamie could make up for any deficiencies in the estate books, Eleanor knew, but the puzzle of where the money had gone bothered him. Eleanor knew it was a problem that Jamie would worry at until he found the solution. He was stubborn like that, just as she was.

She'd thought Jamie would kiss her last evening. Eleanor knew she attracted him, at least sexually; he had made that noticeable on the ride home yesterday though she didn't know what exactly she might have done to cause his... problem.

Eleanor stole a glance at him and sighed. It would be so wrong, but she would have liked a kiss from Jamie. It would be her first kiss and probably her last one, the way her life was turning out. He was adorable, promising to take care of her, but a Duke had too many responsibilities already. Jamie had done enough for her.

It was too early to get a response from any of her inquiries for governess jobs, but Eleanor hoped she would hear soon. The longer time she spent with Jamie, the more her heart would break when she left. Not that he would ever know it, but the vicar's daughter had fallen in love with the Duke, and that was an impossible situation.

There was a knock, and Robert appeared in the doorway. "Your Grace, a coach has arrived."

"Perhaps I should wait here," Eleanor said.

Jamie frowned but nodded. "Perhaps that is best until I see who it is."

He walked out, but Robert lingered. "Would you like a tea tray, Miss Eleanor? I'm sure Cook would ready one for you."

"That would be lovely," Eleanor smiled in gratitude. "The Duke would love biscuits if he isn't delayed too long."

"I didn't recognize the coach, so I thought he'd rather greet them. I spotted them while they were still coming up the drive."

"Oh," responded Eleanor, wondering who it could be. Still, they would all find out. "Well, thank you, Robert."

She resumed her writing, but Robert interrupted once more a few moments later — and without the tea tray.

"The Duke would like to see you in the sitting room, Miss," he said, quivering with excitement. Robert bent down as she passed and hissed at her. "It's the Duchess, Miss Eleanor, come to visit her son."

Oh, Eleanor thought, *a chaperone*. Then she chided herself for her errant thoughts. The Duchess's arrival meant that no improprieties, such as kissing, could occur. It was a better situation for them both.

She followed Robert to the sitting room where an attractive older woman sat on the sofa. She looked much like her son except her hair was blonde. Another gentleman older than Jamie but not middle-aged by his appearance and soberly dressed stood near the fireplace while Jamie remained next to his mother.

Jamie came forward, took Eleanor's hand, and led her to his mother. "Miss Mortimer, I'd like to introduce you to my mother, the Dowager Duchess of Carlisle. Mother, this is Miss Mortimer, whom I wrote to you about."

Eleanor glanced at him, startled. What could he have told the Duchess about her?

The Duchess took Eleanor's hand and pulled her down to sit next to her on the sofa. She smelled of violets, the fine lines around her eyes denoted good humor, and she seemed no more imposing in her title than her son. Eleanor immediately liked her.

"The Duke spoke of you in his letters. I am very sorry for your loss. I did not know your father, but it sounds like he was a lovely man and much respected." She patted Eleanor's hand, and Eleanor blinked, trying to hold back the tears that her kindness brought on. Eleanor did not notice the look she gave her son who had concentrated all his attention on Eleanor, watching her anxiously, his hand flexing as if he needed to reach out and comfort her. The Duchess waited until Eleanor recovered, then looked up to the man standing by the fireplace.

"Miss Mortimer, I would like you to meet the Reverend Mr. Stimpson." The other man in the room came forward and bowed. He was pleasant-looking, his hair thinning, but he had kind eyes. Eleanor realized with a sinking feeling he was there to replace her father. This man would take over her home, and she could never go back now. He seemed to realize it also, that his presence might not be welcome to her at this time and firmed his lips, his face grave.

"Miss Mortimer, I also want to add my condolences on your father's passing. I understand that he was much loved in the parish. It is an honor to follow in his footsteps."

Eleanor nodded stiffly. The Duchess must have realized that Eleanor was close to the limits of her courtesy because her hand tightened on Eleanor's. It was fortunate that Robert wheeled in a tea tray at that point. Eleanor offered, and the Duchess agreed to her pouring the tea. She needed to ask both Mr. Stimpson and the Duchess how they took their tea but handed Jamie a cup made as he liked it. She didn't notice the Duchess's secret smile as Jamie took his teacup and sat down in a chair across from them.

"I like what I have seen of the house very much," the Duchess said to her son. She turned back to Eleanor. "It reminds me of the house I grew up in, Leavens Hall. My brothers and sisters and I ran riot throughout the estate. It was an enjoyable way to grow up."

"Mr. Stimpson, I believe my mother has informed you that you are to live here at Wykeham Hall for the time being." The man nodded as Jamie continued. "Work has begun on the manse, and improvements will be made in both style and size on the house." Eleanor looked up sharply, a pang touching her heart. She hadn't realized that he was changing the house in the rebuilding, and it hurt to think the home she had grown up in would be no more. Still, perhaps that was better. Eleanor was making a clean start. To that end, she would speak to the Duchess about any of her acquaintances that might have an open governess position once the woman relaxed from her trip.

"I am eager to meet my new parishioners. If they are at all like Miss Mortimer in grace and good humor, I shall be most pleased." Mr. Stimpson placed his teacup on the table next to his chair. "Perhaps I can persuade you, Miss Mortimer, to accompany me on visits around the parish to make the first introductions. I would be grateful to have you acquaint me with the people of Sourton." He smiled at Eleanor.

Before she could answer, Jamie put his own teacup down with a rattle. "It will not be necessary to disturb Miss Mortimer, Mr. Stimpson. I shall be glad to accompany you around the area and introduce you to your new church members."

"I hadn't realized that you were so familiar with the area, Your Grace. Your mother indicated that you had newly gained the estate here."

Jamie cleared his throat and leaned forward. "Miss Mortimer has brought me up to speed, and I am prepared to pass my knowledge onto you. There is no need to disturb the lady."

Eleanor blinked. The two men were speaking past her as if she were an inanimate object, like a pillow tossed on the sofa. They were like two little boys fighting over a favorite toy, not allowing her to speak for herself, and she found it unsettling.

The Duchess finally interrupted the men's squabbling. "Miss Mortimer will be busy with me."

All three of them looked at her, waiting for her to go on. Eleanor wondered what the Duchess had in mind, but the older woman changed the subject. "For now, though, I believe I will find my way to my room and have a rest before dinnertime. Elise should have put away my things by now."

She rose, and the men leaped to their feet, Eleanor following slowly, still bewildered by the previous conversation. The Duchess turned to her. "Would you be so kind as to show me to my chamber, Miss Mortimer?"

Eleanor took the woman's arm and led her to the stairs. She was most perplexed. Behind her, she heard Jamie give Robert orders to show Mr. Stimpson to his room. He was not staying in the family wing. She should have moved from there also once the Duke arrived, but no one had thought it. Perhaps she should suggest a move, but then she wouldn't be here much longer if a job came through. They ascended the stairs, Eleanor conscious of Jamie's heavier tread following them.

Eleanor led the Duchess to the apartment next to the Duke's that she knew Mrs. Makepeace had readied for her use. It had a small sitting room with the adjoining bedroom. The Baron's young wife had died many years before, but they had always kept the room pristine as if waiting for her return. Eleanor wasn't sure a Duchess would find it suitable, but this particular Duchess didn't seem very high in the instep.

In fact, the Duchess surveyed the room and clapped her hands. "Lovely," she said. "Very much like my mother's room at Leavens. Don't you think so, darling?"

Eleanor was very conscious of Jamie standing behind her.

"I remember little about the Countess's suite or if I was ever in the rooms, but I will take your word for it. I agree the house has the feel of Leavens." Jamie walked by her, and Eleanor breathed a sigh of relief. She much preferred having the Duke where she could keep him in her sight.

"I'll leave you to talk together or rest if you will," Eleanor said with a curtsey and fled for the door. Once in the hallway, she was at a loss where she should go next. She didn't want to linger outside the Duchess's suite, but she also did not care to go to her own room down the hall. She should go back to copying letters for the Duke, but Eleanor did not think he would come back soon. Mother and son must have confidences to share.

She decided to take a walk outside. Stretching her legs would feel good, and while the day wasn't sunny, it was clear with a slight breeze. Eleanor escaped to the gardens, intending to walk down to a wooded copse on the far side of the lawn where there was a gazebo under the trees. Like most all the outside buildings, it was in need of paint, but she had taken a book out there a few times and found it private and comfortable.

The walk made her feel better though it wasn't enough. Eleanor was restless, at odds with herself. Her time at Wykeham Hall was ending. The new vicar had arrived, and she couldn't return to the manse again. The Duke and his mother would soon travel to another of their many estates or houses.

And she? Eleanor would live with a strange family, teaching their small children.

Never to see Jamie again.

Chapter Ten

"James, what a lovely woman Miss Mortimer is. I like her very much." The Duchess sat in a damask-covered chair in her suite and motioned for Jamie to join her. "I suspect that she will make a very suitable wife for Mr. Stimpson."

Jamie tugged at the cuffs of his shirt under his jacket sleeve. His mother refused to call her only child by his title. In private, he was always James, and she was Mama.

He answered carefully as his mother was no fool. "I suspect Miss Mortimer would make an excellent wife for any man." He didn't look up as his cuffs needed more of an adjustment than he expected. It had nothing to do with not wanting to meet his mother's eyes. She knew him better than anyone, even Lucy, and Jamie did not want to give anything away yet. Therefore, he missed the look of amusement and love that passed over his mother's face.

"Well, I primed Mr. Stimpson. I dropped subtle hints in the carriage on the way here, and he is disposed to look favorably on Miss Mortimer."

Jamie looked up swiftly. "What manner of man is he? What is his family background?"

"Mr. Stimpson is from an appropriate family related to me somewhat distantly. He was an assistant to a vicar in a large parish in northern Cumbria and is eager to have his own congregation."

Jamie sat back in his chair with a disgruntled huff. While he wanted a good man for the vicar of Sourton, he wanted to find a few flaws that would make the person unattractive to Eleanor as a potential husband.

He worried that the appeal of remaining among her acquaintances and familiar friends would overcome any temptation to Eleanor of becoming a Duchess. It was a genuine possibility. Wealth or position wouldn't entice Eleanor. He chewed on his thumb while he pondered what would beguile Eleanor, forgetting his mother who was observing him with a raised eyebrow.

"James, is something the matter with Mr. Stimpson? I tried to match your requirements for a vicar and possible husband for Miss Mortimer. He seems suitable in both respects."

Caught, he shook his head. "No, I'm sure he is adequate." He arose and crossed over to give his mother a kiss on the forehead. "Thank you very much for reconnoitering for me. You would have made an excellent general under Wellington.

"I'll let you rest now. I appreciate the speed with you undertook this journey as I feared to put Miss Mortimer in an awkward position, and the lady has no other recourse."

The Duchess reached out and took Jamie's hand, giving it a squeeze and a pat. "You know I will always do whatever you need from me."

He nodded and walked away when she called, "And James."

Jamie turned back, the smile still on his face that being with his mother always brought. "Yes?"

"You can talk to me about anything, you know."

He tensed but gave her a nod. "When I'm ready, Mama, you will be the first one I come to. I always value your advice. Meanwhile, any aid you might give Miss Mortimer would be much appreciated, I'm sure."

He walked out of the room, not seeing his mother watch him leave with a huge smile on her face.

JAMIE STRODE DOWN THE hallway to the office, hoping that Eleanor had returned there. He was not sure where Mr. Stimpson was, though presumably, he was in his room acquainting himself with his new surroundings. Mrs. Makepeace had wanted to put him in the family wing, but she had not objected when Jamie had suggested the guest wing of the house. Jamie's male instinct said Reverend Stimpson should be as far away from Eleanor as possible at all times.

He had noted the man's interest when Eleanor had walked into the sitting room. A vicar who had his own parish would next want a wife, a helpmate to aid him in his clerical duties. Who better than the attractive vicar's daughter who already knew everyone in the area? Jamie ground his teeth as he walked into the office.

Which was empty.

Where was Eleanor? He was sure she had not gone to her own room to rest. She was much too active a person though that scenario put the thought into Jamie's head of he and Eleanor both taking 'naps' together in the afternoon at a point in the future, hopefully soon. He felt a stirring and pushed that idea out of his mind. Eleanor had already seen more than a gently bred woman should on the carriage ride back from Okehampton.

He backed out of the office and strode back to the main hall. Perhaps Robert knew where Eleanor was. Instead, he ran into Anna, one of the maids who was wheeling the tea cart back towards the kitchen. He hadn't sorted out the staff completely, but he knew Anna because she had lent Eleanor her dress.

"Have you seen Miss Mortimer?" he asked her. Anna was a plain girl, but pleasant, and Eleanor said she was good at her duties.

She curtsied and replied, "Yes, Your Grace. Miss Mortimer is out in the gardens. I saw her go out there earlier."

"Thank you." Jamie headed for the outdoors.

Eleanor wasn't in the gardens, and Jamie turned in a circle, trying to determine where she might have gone. Eleanor would not have taken a horse out, even with a groom. He had been taking her for short rides, and her riding was improving, but she was still too unsure of herself to have hacked out on her own. The estate grounds were not that large though he supposed she could have tried to walk to the village. Yet Anna had said she was in the gardens, and she would have left word if she had left the grounds.

Jamie slowly circled, looking in all directions and finally spied her black dress in the little gazebo down below the gardens. The building needed repairs and Jamie had tasked Mr. Brown with finding a carpenter, but the job was much further down on the list of needed improvements to the estate.

He set off in a long stride, determined to find Eleanor and... what? His mind was a muddle of jealousy, fear, and longing.

She watched him approach. Jamie could not determine from her expression whether or not she was happy to see him. He hesitated; perhaps she sought solitude, and he should let her be. Eleanor broke into a smile, and Jamie felt the warmth of it to his very marrow. Whether or not she wanted solitude, she did not mind him being there.

"Eleanor," he said as he reached her, and Jamie savored her name on his lips.

"It must thrill you that your mother has arrived." Eleanor smoothed a wrinkle in the skirt of the black gown she wore and then looked up at him. "Do you see her often?"

"We are close, especially since my father died. I depend on her greatly, and I esteem her advice."

"She is a lovely lady and the first Duchess I have ever met," Eleanor said.

Jamie laughed and sat on the rickety stairs leading up to the platform where Eleanor sat.

"My mother is a remarkable woman. I'm very proud of her." Jamie picked a leaf off one of the bushes surrounding the building and folded it over and over. "She and my father loved each other deeply. She was heartbroken when he died, but she kept going and helped her confused and grieving son, suddenly thrust into a role he was not prepared to assume."

At Eleanor's puzzled look, he continued, "I was trained to become a Duke; my father saw to it. I just wasn't ready to be on my own, to have the responsibility of hundreds of people thrust upon me."

"But you've learned," Eleanor responded. "I've seen how hard you work, how you deal with your people. I don't believe there is another Duke in the whole of England as responsible as you."

Jamie felt the tips of his ears get hot. He was absurdly pleased with Eleanor's compliments.

"Thank you. I try my best," he answered. He tore the leaf in his hand into little pieces. "My mother liked you also."

Eleanor protested, "She doesn't even know me."

"Ah, but she is splendid at first impressions and an excellent judge of character." Jamie looked away across the lawns. "Also, she might have heard about you from me."

"Oh, dear," Eleanor teased, leaning forward toward to where he sat on the steps. "Then she must think the worst of me."

"No," Jamie said fiercely, and Eleanor pulled back in surprise. Jamie modulated his tone. "Your pardon, but I have only ever warmly spoken of you." He threw the pieces of the leaf down on the ground and wiped his hands on his breeches.

Eleanor didn't speak, and Jamie decided it was best to change the subject. "My mother would like it if you could accompany her about the country on some visits to the local gentry. We would understand if you felt that your mourning prevents that activity, but Mama would find it very helpful if you could see your way."

Eleanor hesitated but shrugged and said, "Of course. My father was always a practical man. I do not believe he would begrudge me helping the Duchess. It's not as if I were attending dances, after all."

"Thank you, Eleanor. That means a great deal to us. I don't know what we would do without your aid."

Eleanor shook her head. "Now that is doing it up too brown. You are a Duke, and your mother is a Duchess. I know that you both manage just fine on your own and don't need me to help you." She laughed. "I wouldn't know where to begin if I had to do the things you and your mother accomplish as a matter of course."

"You act the role naturally, Eleanor. It is a part of your essence. You could be a Duchess tomorrow." Jamie wondered if Eleanor would catch the hidden meaning to his words, but if she did, she ignored it.

"I will be a governess, if not tomorrow, but soon. That is the role I will play in life."

"What if you had another option?"

Eleanor looked puzzled but intrigued. "Like what?" she asked.

Jamie shrugged, trying to appear casual although his heart was beating through his chest. "Marriage." He looked up at the house, not able to bear to see the look on her face if she was rejecting him.

There was a long pause. "Marriage is not in the cards for me, Your Grace." She stood, and Jamie bounded to his feet though he wanted to curl into a ball and howl. He would play the gentleman yet.

"I believe I will rest before dinner." Jamie stayed silent and held out a hand to help Eleanor down the steps. The contact of her hand was almost too much for him. He wanted to pull her into his arms and kiss her until she agreed to marry him. Jamie's breeding carried him through. He escorted her back to the house, neither of them speaking for the length of the march up the lawn to the front door.

Robert greeted them at the door. For once, Jamie thought, he was staffing his position at the front entrance. "Your Grace, Miss Mortimer, some packages have arrived for you from Okehampton. I wasn't sure where to put them."

Eleanor smiled. "That would be my purchases..." Her voice trailed off as she spotted the pile of boxes wrapped in brown paper. "This can't all be for me."

"No, Miss Mortimer," Robert answered and pulled one small package that looked like books off of the pile. "This one is for His Grace."

Eleanor wheeled on Jamie, her eyes flashing with indignation.

"Your Grace, this is not acceptable," she sputtered.

"Miss Mortimer, I cannot have you accompanying my mother in rags. *That* is what would not be acceptable.

Eleanor's shoulders slumped in resignation, and Jamie felt better. His Eleanor was a stubborn woman, but he had outwitted her once. He would come up with a better plan to entice her into marriage.

Chapter Eleven

Robert carried the packages up to her room, and Eleanor set about inspecting the contents. The Duke had made arrangements with Mrs. Glass that far outstripped what Eleanor had expected. She tried to be indignant but was too grateful to maintain her choler.

There were delicate underthings, unlike the practical garments she wore under her clothing. They made her blush, then laugh as she thought of shy Jamie asking Mrs. Glass about them. There were several gowns, two in black, but the others were in shades of gray, mauve, and one that was a dark, dark blue. They would be suitable for when she was in half-mourning and would work well for a governess. There was a beautiful green silk shawl, two bonnets, stockings, and a new pair of half-boots that were her size though she did not know how Jamie had got the right measurements as Mrs. Glass had not looked at her feet.

There was also the most extravagant item of all. Jamie had made good on his threat, and there was a dark green riding habit complete with a bonnet that had a jaunty pheasant feather. Eleanor marveled at the fit. Mrs. Glass and her girls must have been sewing for the last few days to have accomplished all this.

It was all too much. Eleanor tried to be firm, but she reasoned that Jamie was correct when he said she needed the clothes to accompany his mother on her rounds. If she considered that the garments were a gift from the Duchess, then she could accept them graciously, even if her thinking was a little specious and self-serving.

Eleanor sat down heavily in the chair in her bedroom, the tail of the habit trailing across the floor. What had Jamie meant when he pressed her about marriage? She knew he didn't like the idea of her taking a governess position, but the way he said it and then looked to the house where Mr. Stimpson was standing in the window watching them made it seem as if he had other plans.

Mr. Stimpson appeared to be a nice man, but Eleanor did not know him. She was certainly not going to marry him, but she could see how Jamie might think it a good idea. Eleanor would no longer be his responsibility, and he would consider it a perfect solution to have her live in her old home and village. It angered her at first he would be so blind as to suggest that she marry Mr. Stimpson. Yes, it solved her difficulties, but Jamie was not usually so insensitive. It made her sad.

Lost in thought, Eleanor almost missed the knock on her door. When she called out to enter, Anna poked her head in the door. They had known each other for a while but had become friendly during Eleanor's sojourn at Wykeham Hall.

"Miss Eleanor, I heard you received packages," she said in excitement. Eleanor waved for her to enter, and Anna came into the room only to gape in amazement as she saw what Eleanor was wearing.

"Oh, that's lovely, Miss Eleanor. That color looks good on you, pardon my saying so, but with you in mourning and all." Anna was fingering the hem of the jacket. "You know, miss, we are not so strict about wearing colors here in the country as in London." Anna glimpsed the matching hat and went over to retrieve it. Anna had dreams of becoming a ladies maid and pored over the newspapers for pictures of the latest fashions. She brought the bonnet over and placed it carefully on Eleanor's curls, tilting it slightly forward over her eyes.

"There, that's perfect. You look so fashionable, just like a Duchess, I imagine." Anna stepped back and surveyed Eleanor's outfit, but her words diverted Eleanor.

"I'm not a Duchess, Anna."

Anna shook her head. "You could be. I've seen the way the Duke looks at you. You would make a wonderful Duchess. I imagine it's not that different from marrying a vicar."

Eleanor laughed, not unkindly, but amused by Anna's pronouncement. "I think it is very different. A Duchess must move about in society, do good works, and manage the Duke's households."

"And isn't that what you did for the vicar, miss? Oh, maybe the people here aren't so high and mighty, but you still had to deal with them for the vicar." Anna sniffed. "Those noble folk put their pants on one leg at a time, same as us poorer folks."

Anna spied the other dresses on the bed where Eleanor had tossed them and hung them up in the wardrobe, cooing the entire time, while Eleanor disrobed.

"It's almost time for dinner, miss. What do you want to wear this evening?" Anna determined to act as Eleanor's lady's maid. Eleanor didn't need one, but she hated to upset Anna, who was kind to her.

"I don't know. Why don't you pick out a dress? One of the black gowns," she replied.

"May I do your hair too, Miss Eleanor? I've been practicing on Bessie, and her hair is not near as pretty as yours." At Eleanor's look, she added, "It won't be too fancy, I promise. It'll suit you."

Eleanor agreed, wondering what she had gotten herself into.

ELEANOR PAUSED OUTSIDE the sitting room where the others had gathered before dinner. Meals at Wykeham Hall would be more formal affairs now that there were others beside Jamie and Eleanor to dine. She smoothed her hands down the front of her dress. It had been a struggle, but she had talked Anna into one of the black gowns. The material was excellent, and the bodice cut a bit lower than she was used to. Anna refused to let her wear a fichu, so she had the locket that her mother had bequeathed her instead, though it did not cover her chest the way she liked. Anna had wound a black velvet ribbon through her curls after piling them on her head in a manner that both ladies thought made Eleanor look softer. Still, she was nervous.

She had thought about what Anna said about a Duchess's duties compared to a vicar's wife, and in some respects, the maid was correct. It was a matter of the front one put forward because the core responsibilities were the same, just different degrees of rank. Jamie was attracted to her, and she was in love with him. Eleanor didn't want to let her fancies fly too far, but just maybe Anna was right.

No more time to dawdle, she thought. Eleanor straightened her spine and lifted her chin. She could hear the murmur of conversation which stopped as she walked into the room. The Duchess smiled, Mr. Stimpson nodded, but Jamie looked gob-smacked. An inner tension in Eleanor relaxed at the sight of his gaping before he pulled himself together to come to greet her and escort her into the room.

"My dear, how lovely you look," the Duchess nodded her approval. Eleanor curtsied, dipping carefully, but she blushed as she heard Jamie inhale loudly. Even Mr. Stimpson blinked and stared at her display of bosom, an indiscreet gesture for a clergyman. Eleanor was torn; while she was glad that Jamie seemed to approve, she did not want to encourage Mr. Stimpson if he thought to make a match.

She sat next to the Duchess as they waited for the dinner gong to sound. While she and Jamie had not been so formal, Eleanor had attended enough dinners as guests with her father she was used to the ritual.

Jamie was still standing, and Eleanor saw how handsome he looked in his formal clothes. He had dressed in black also except for a snowy white cravat, and his auburn hair shone over the broadcloth that fit his frame so well. Mr. Stimpson looked positively dowdy in his sober suit. The Duchess was in a formal dinner gown of a lavender color that set off the silver blonde in her hair.

"His Grace explained your circumstances with the disaster at the manse. How dreadful to have a tree crash down like that and how lucky that you were not seriously injured. I am so sorry that your possessions were destroyed though and thrilled that we could accommodate your new wardrobe."

Eleanor heaved out a sigh of relief. The Duchess had nicely explained the new clothing and taken credit for helping Eleanor without directly involving the Duke. It was a worry that Eleanor had tried to bury. People would gossip, and some might even take it as a reason she must marry the Duke since he bought her such personal items. Eleanor hoped to marry Jamie, but she didn't want him to feel coerced.

Robert sounded the dinner gong, and Mr. Stimpson was at her side in a flash. "Please let me escort you to dinner, Miss Mortimer."

Eleanor glanced at Jamie, but he was taking his mother's arm as precedence required. She took Mr. Stimpson's arm, and they followed them into the dining room.

Mrs. Makepeace had made a good showing. The linens gleaming snow-white and the china shone in the candlelight. The table was a bit long for four people, but she must have consulted the Duke, and the settings were all placed at one end, a bit informal but much more suitable for conversation while dining. Mr. Stimpson put her on Jamie's left and sat down on the other side of her while the Duchess took a place on Jamie's right.

Robert served them soup, a flavorful chicken broth. Jamie would have to employ more footmen or a butler if he intended to do more entertaining while he was here, Eleanor thought. Poor Robert could just about handle the four of them though she supposed that one of the maids could be pressed into service if necessary. Eleanor couldn't imagine a life where too few servants were a problem.

Mr. Stimpson asked her about the manse. Eleanor had recovered enough composure she could answer.

"It was a comfortable home, Mr. Stimpson, though I understand that the Duke is expanding it. I'm sure you'll find the living arrangements will more than satisfy you. It is also in a very convenient location, private, but near enough to the church and village."

"I understand the manse is being prepared for a family." Mr. Stimpson gave Eleanor an unctuous leer that made Eleanor pull back in surprise. She glanced at the Duke and his mother, who seemed to watch fascinated as Mr. Stimpson took another spoonful of soup.

"I did not know you had a family," Eleanor responded politely. "Are they following shortly?"

"Alas, I do not have a family—yet," he said with another leer that made Eleanor regret the neckline of her dress. The Duke coughed.

"I mean to say my fiancée passed on, and I must find another if I am to wed."

Eleanor blinked and looked at the Duchess who did not seem affected by this sad news.

"I am very sorry for your loss. Was it recent?"

Eleanor wished that Jamie or his mother would join the conversation because she needed some help here. She didn't know what to make of this strange man. He was the Duchess's choice for a vicar, and she respected the Dowager Duchess. The man must be qualified, but he was a little odd.

"She will burn in the fires of Hell."

Eleanor dropped her spoon, and Jamie began to cough. He grasped his wine goblet, taking a hearty swig, and hid his face behind the rim. The Duchess continued to sip her soup, a tiny smile marking the edge of her lips.

"I beg your pardon, Miss Mortimer. But Emma is an evil woman and deserves to punishment."

Eleanor squeaked, "Surely, she deserves God's forgiveness, Mr. Stimpson, no matter her sins." She swallowed and continued. "What did she die of?"

"She is not dead. Why would you think that?"

Jamie put his cup down, staring at his new vicar in amazement. Eleanor waved her hands and tried not to sputter.

"I thought you said she passed on," Eleanor asked, trying to understand this strange conversation.

"She did. She passed on to York with Mr. Browning, the tanner. Chose him over me. Left a note." Mr. Stimpson shook his head and applied himself to the last of his soup.

Eleanor hastily pulled her napkin up from her lap to cover her laughter. Jamie's face was bright red with suppressed amusement, but the Duchess only betrayed mirth by a slight pink rosiness in her cheeks.

Mr. Stimpson lifted his head from his soup bowl and sat back, patting his stomach. "So you see, Miss Mortimer, I am in need of a wife."

Instantly, Jamie's smile turned to a glower. He finally entered the conversation.

"I wish you well in your search, Mr. Stimpson. There are several fine young ladies in the neighborhood we will try to bring to your notice."

The Dowager Duchess continued to smile pleasantly.

Chapter Twelve

Jamie could have his morning ride with Eleanor despite the threatening rain. She looked glorious in her new riding habit. She was a cautious rider, and they did not go far, but Jamie found that just a little time with Eleanor soothed his ruffled soul.

Mr. Stimpson had irritated him beyond belief with his suggestions and his leering glances the previous evening. Jamie had got through the hours just barely but had confronted his mother when he escorted her to her bedchamber.

"What were you thinking?"

His mother's eyes were just a little too wide to display real innocence. "About what, darling?"

"Mr. Stimpson! Is he truly suitable for the vicar in Sourton?"

"Well, he's a bit enthusiastic, but the bishop assured me he performs his duties as minister admirably." The Duchess seated herself in one of the delicate chairs in her boudoir and straightened her skirts, not looking up at her son. "He seems eager to find a wife, and that was your other requirement," she said mildly.

Jamie paused. Perhaps this was the time to confide in her and enlist his mother's aid in his marital quest. "What if I did not wish Mr. Stimpson to marry Miss Mortimer any longer? Perhaps we should find him another young lady."

"But what of Miss Mortimer? She spoke of a governess position at one point, but that is not suitable for a woman of her kindness and gentility." His mother smiled at him, a genuine smile, and Jamie heaved out a sigh of relief. His mother understood him and was in perfect agreement.

"I'm sure we will find her the perfect position," he answered and kissed her on the cheek.

Now he was in the cabriolet with Mr. Stimpson, taking him on a tour of the village. The new vicar didn't ride, so Jamie drove with him in the carriage. Still, he knew his duty. And if the trip took him to the Beaton's home where Mr. Stimpson could meet Miss Beaton, then the few hours together this morning would not be wasted.

Jamie had grown used to Eleanor's calm presence. Mr. Stimpson was a chatterer, going on about his past position, his ex-fiancee, and the marvels he was discovering in Devon. He was in raptures when they stopped to inspect the work being done on the manse. Jamie couldn't begrudge him. Every honest man wanted a home of his own and a position of respect. It surprised him when Stimpson made several good suggestions about the construction and then ashamed of himself for misjudging the man, at least in this regard.

They stopped for lunch at the Highwayman Inn, and Jamie introduced the new rector to Mr. Rawlings and several other men who were in the taproom. The rain looked to be holding off, so they continued on to the Beaton home. On the way, Jamie extolled the virtues of Miss Beaton to Mr. Stimpson. He may have exaggerated slightly, but no one would blame him for that as he hardly knew the woman.

It was a large house, suitable for a wealthy merchant family. Mrs. Beaton and her daughter were pleased that the Duke had come for a visit and happy to be the first family of the local gentry to meet the new vicar. Mrs. Beaton was a practical woman, and almost immediately she set her sights on Stimpson for her unmarried daughter. She had to know she had no hope of snagging a Duke for the girl, anyway.

Mr. Stimpson was polite and conversed with Miss Beaton, leaving Jamie to talk with the mother. He thought matters were progressing well until Mrs. Beaton asked him about Eleanor.

"For I must confess, Your Grace, that it quite surprised me to see you with Miss Mortimer in Okehampton last week."

Mr. Stimpson, unfortunately, chose this moment to insert himself into their conversation. "Why surprising, Mrs. Beaton? Miss Mortimer has been living at Wykeham Hall these many weeks since the storm destroyed the manse."

The woman's eyes gleamed, and Jamie moved quickly to stem her perchance for gossip. "Mrs. Makepeace, the housekeeper, has been acting as chaperone since Miss Mortimer did not expect my arrival. Now my mother, the Dowager Duchess of Carlisle has arrived, and all is entirely proper."

"Of course, of course, Your Grace," observed Mrs. Beaton. "I would not suggest otherwise."

The men took their leave after that, but Jamie was uneasy. Mrs. Beaton could make trouble if she chose. She was not a stupid woman and if she wanted to remove Miss Mortimer from Mr. Stimpson's grasp to promote her own daughter, forcing Jamie into marriage with Eleanor would be a good solution. Not that Jamie opposed marrying Eleanor — that was his goal — but he wanted it to be of her free will.

The rain finally broke as they came through the village. Jamie had put up the roof, but it wasn't much protection against the slanting rain off the Devon moors. It chilled the two men and soaked them to the skin by the time they reached Wykeham Hall.

Jamie went at once to his suite and stripped, shivering in the cool air. Already he had a headache, and his throat felt sore, but he determined to carry on. Some hot tea and a tot of brandy should put him to rights.

He managed through dinner, determined not to leave Eleanor alone with Mr. Stimpson. His mother had taken a tray in her room for her evening meal. Jamie's eyes felt increasingly bleary although Stimpson seemed hale, not sick at all. By the meal's end, Jamie was forced to retire to his own bed as he could barely stay awake. Perhaps an early night would see him well in the morning.

Bates came in to dress him for his morning ride and immediately informed the Duke that he was too feverish to go out and must stay in bed for the day. Jamie protested, not wanting to miss time with Eleanor, but Bates cheated and called the Duchess in, who took one look at her ashen-faced son and put her foot down. By this time, Jamie could barely lift his head from his pillow. He alternated between chills and fever.

The Duchess sent for the doctor, but it seemed he was away in Bath and wouldn't be back for two days. Worried, she consulted Eleanor as Jamie got worse.

Jamie knew of Eleanor standing with his mother at his bedside. He moaned when she placed a cold cloth on his forehead, hardly comprehending as he heard her say, "I will act as nurse to His Grace. I had often taken care of the villagers' needs when they were hurt or ill."

"I confess I am very anxious about his state," the Duchess said. "His Grace has a strong constitution, and though I've sent to Bath to alert the doctor, I fear my son's needs are more urgent right now."

"It is just as well that Mr. Stimpson did not take ill." Their voices faded away as Jamie returned to sleep. He occasionally woke for sips of water, but mostly he dreamed. He talked to his father, walking beside him as a man now instead of the child he had been when his father passed away. Lydia scorned him once again to marry her elderly Duke, but Jamie didn't mind. He only felt a sense of relief as he watched her walk away until her blonde hair turned to brown and he realized it was Eleanor leaving him behind.

He called out, "Eleanor, stay!" in a hoarse voice and calmed when a hand soothed his brow and he heard her murmur, "I'm here, Jamie, don't fret." Frantic, he grasped her hand and wouldn't release it even when he fell back asleep, holding it as a lifeline. If he let go, she would leave him.

Jamie could hear others around his bed. Bates and his mother conferred and tried to talk Eleanor into leaving so she could get some rest. He tried to protest. He was dreadfully afraid that if Eleanor left, he would not see her again. She would go away from him to become a governess. Mr. Stimpson prayed over him, his voice resonant and comforting. *Perhaps his mother was correct, and the man was a decent vicar*, Jamie thought as he drifted off again.

Throughout his illness, one constant remained: Elanor. She seemed to be there almost always, but if she stepped away and Jamie was somewhat conscious, he would call for her. Jamie knew it should embarrass him at his display of weakness, but he didn't care. He wanted Eleanor's cool hands wiping down his body during fits of fever, her soft remonstrance in his ear as she worked over him. Bates rolled him over so Eleanor could change the linens. Jamie knew he was naked, and that Bates had undressed him to help with keeping him cool. Eleanor, as a maiden lady, shouldn't attend him, but he was helpless to protest.

Jamie woke in candlelight, freezing again. His whole body shivered, shaking the bed. Eleanor's head and arms were lying across the coverlet. She had fallen asleep in her chair next to the bed where she had been keeping watch.

"Eleanor," Jamie called, his teeth chattering. He hated to wake her when she was so tired, but he had no choice. He needed the chamber pot.

She lifted her head, eyes bleary, but alert in an instant. "Jamie, are you awake? What on earth...?"

"I'm terribly sorry, but can you call Bates for me? I need to use the facilities."

"Oh, of course. He's sleeping on the sofa in your antechamber." She rose, tucking curls back behind her ears. Her hair was in a long braid down her back.

In a minute, Bates was there, rubbing his eyes, but prepared to help Jamie to the privacy screen and then back to the bed. Jamie was exhausted, relieved to empty his bladder, but still shivering.

"Let me get Miss Eleanor, Your Grace," Bates said in a worried tone.

"No, let her get some rest. I just need another blanket."

Bates shook his head. "Miss Eleanor will have my hide if I don't get her, milord. She is strict about your care, and I dare not cross her." He left the room before Jamie could say anything more. He slumped back on his pillow and waited.

Eleanor came in, her face drawn with weariness. She smiled when she saw him, though, and that warmed Jamie just a little.

"Would you like another sip of water? You need to drink as much as you can," she said as she approached with a glass. "Oh dear, your teeth are chattering!"

"Cold," Jamie agreed, closing his eyes. He could hear her moving around the room over the noise of his teeth, and then a coverlet was smoothed over his body. It helped, but he still shivered.

"Cold," he repeated. He held up a corner of the blanket. "Warm me." In some part of his mind, Jamie knew what he'd said was scandalous, but he didn't care. He would marry Eleanor, and he was cold, and she needed to rest.

He heard her sigh, but then the mattress sank as she climbed into the bed. Although he was still under most of the blankets, and she was on top, but Jamie could feel her body heat through the layers. He snuggled against her like a child with his mother. Jamie was still too ill to have licentious thoughts; he wanted the comfort of her against him. He could plead delirium if necessary.

ELEANOR WAS TOASTY warm, something heavy across her waist, and a warm breath on the back of her neck when she awakened as several people entered the room. She opened her eyes to see Bates and the doctor who had finally arrived. Behind him was the Duchess and Mr. Stimpson, his mouth open in horror.

That was when she realized that she was lying in Jamie's bed, and it was his arm across her middle. She flung the offending limb away as she scrambled to get off the bed and away from him. He was stirring, scratching at his face as he tried to sit up against his pillows. Jamie still looked pale, but his eyes were brighter, and his fever had broken. He didn't seem awake yet though or understand what had just happened. The doctor gave Eleanor an incredulous look but bustled over to the bed to examine the Duke. The Dowager Duchess smiled sympathetically at Eleanor but followed the doctor over to see her son.

Eleanor rushed out of the room, appalled at what had happened. Mr. Stimpson followed her out and called to her before she could leave the Duke's sitting room.

"Miss Mortimer, I must speak to you."

Eleanor stopped and turned to face the vicar. One look at his face and she knew he had decided her fate.

Chapter Thirteen

Jamie woke up confused. He was feeling better though very thirsty. He wasn't sure why Eleanor had rushed out of the room, followed by Mr. Stimpson, but he didn't like it. The scene was much too close to his fever dream.

Once he realized the man fussing over him was the long-lost doctor, he had a better idea of what had occurred. Jamie was weak as a kitten, but he could remember some of the night's events. Bates was making faces and gestures behind the doctor and his mother that also reminded him. Eleanor! He had coaxed her into bed with him, just for comfort and warmth. She had still been curled up next to him when the mob of visitors had charged into his bedroom.

"I'm all right, quite recovered," Jamie blurted out at the doctor and attempted to arise from his bed, forgetting he was naked under the bedclothes. He needed to find Eleanor right away. The way she had darted out of the room was disturbing. The doctor was a small man, but he pushed Jamie right back into the bed as the illness had left him weaker than he thought.

"Mama," Jamie pleaded with his mother.

"You stay right there, young man, and let the doctor do his duty." She softened, relieved that her son was feeling better. "I'll check on Eleanor."

Jamie flopped back against his pillows and rolled his eyes at Bates, who just shrugged. The doctor poured a noxious-looking liquid into a glass on the bedroom table and held it out to Jamie.

"Drink this, Your Grace."

Jamie pursed his lips, about to tell the late-arriving doctor what to do with his drink when Bates shook his head. If he wanted to get rid of the man, he should do as he was told. He took the glass and drank it down.

"Pshawwww."

MR. STIMPSON LOOKED stern. Eleanor took a deep breath, trying to get her errant curls back into the braid or at least behind her ears.

"Miss Mortimer," the vicar began. "While I understand that you are performing a good deed in nursing the Duke, it is not acceptable for an unmarried woman of good morals to be lying in his bed." The vicar blushed, but Eleanor paled. This could not be happening. She had been so careful until now, but last night she was tired, and Jamie couldn't get warm. She had been so worried about Jamie's sickness and just wanted a little comfort from him. But not compromising. She had meant to get up when he fell back asleep but must have succumbed to her tiredness.

Mr. Stimpson took her hand. "I understand that nothing untoward occurred, but, it does not look good. I must speak to the Duke."

"What! Why?" Eleanor was much too tired for this encounter. She could see her life crumbling away in front of her.

"My dear Miss Mortimer, in the absence of your father, I will stand in to protect your rights. Of course, the Duke will do the right thing, but it is my duty..."

"No, no, no, no!" With each word, Eleanor's voice rose. "I am sure that is unnecessary, Mr. Stimpson. There is absolutely no reason it need concern the Duke. I understand that this incident was just an accident, and there is no reason for a bother."

Mr. Stimpson shook his head. "I don't think you understand the gravity of the situation for yourself. For myself, knowing your good character, I could overlook this mishap. But the doctor and now the other servants know you spent the night in the Duke's room."

"I was just nursing him!" Eleanor was near tears. How could this have happened?

There was a rustling, and the Duchess appeared in the doorway behind the vicar. Eleanor wasn't sure how much she heard, but she had to believe the Duchess would want her son to have a wife of equal rank and background. Surely she would help Eleanor out of this contretemps.

"Mr. Stimpson, please let me speak to Miss Mortimer if you please. I believe I can work out a suitable solution to this dilemma." Mr. Stimpson looked as if he wanted to protest, but he bowed and walked out of the room.

"Come with me please," the Duchess ordered and walked to the inner door that connected the two suites. Eleanor followed her, feeling somewhat relieved. The Duchess must be as appalled as she was herself. She wouldn't let Eleanor marry her son.

Eleanor wanted Jamie to want to marry her, but not forced to it. She would never know if he genuinely cared for her if they compelled him. She would rather not marry him if it was under duress.

The Duchess sat in one of the chairs in her antechamber and Eleanor took the other. She twisted her hands together, nervous, but waited for the Duchess to speak first.

The other woman studied her carefully, her eyes kind and Eleanor relaxed. Intuitively, she felt that the Duchess was on her side, maybe for different reasons, but Jamie's mother would help her out of this mess.

"Miss Mortimer, would it be all right if I called you Eleanor?"

"Of course, Your Grace. I would consider it an honor."

"This title business is a bother, at least in a personal context." She shook her head but then seemed to collect herself. "Firstly, thank you for your contributions in bringing my son back to health. I believe he has a way to go, but he is much improved this morning, and that is due to your efforts."

Eleanor sagged a little, relieved to hear the Duchess's words. She had not stayed long enough to know Jamie was feeling better. Her impression had been that his fever had abated, but she didn't know for sure.

"I'm glad, Your Grace. His Grace has been most kind, and I am happy to help in the small way I can," Eleanor responded. She wanted to hear the Duchess' solution for avoiding being compromised which was why it shocked her to hear her next words.

"You will be an excellent helpmate to my son, Eleanor, and a fine Duchess. I'm very pleased though the circumstances might be better. Still, it is what it is. I will arrange for a special license sent here as Carlisle is too weak to attend to any business for now. We wouldn't want him to have a relapse with a wedding imminent."

"But Your Grace," gasped Eleanor. "There can be no marriage. This is a mistake. I fell asleep by accident. Jamie, I mean the Duke doesn't want to marry me. I'm not suitable." She was wringing her hands in her distress, but the Duchess looked unmoved.

"Eleanor, of course, you will marry my son. If he were feeling better, he would assure you of this himself. As it falls to me, I want to assure you that you are eminently suitable to be the Duchess of Carlisle. You are a gentlewoman of education and good manners. You are organized, and already you help Carlisle with the business of the Duchy. And the two of you spent the night together."

She held up a hand as Eleanor tried to protest again. "I know that nothing untoward occurred. Frankly, it was only because my son was too ill. I've seen the way you look at each other, and I know that you find each other attractive."

Eleanor put her hands on her hot cheeks as if that would hide her embarrassment. There was a sinking feeling in her stomach, a rock with jagged edges roiling around until she thought she might be sick.

"Your Grace," she spoke with quiet dignity. "I esteem His Grace greatly, but that is all the more reason we wouldn't suit. The Ton will laugh him at for being trapped by a simple country girl and tear his reputation apart."

The Duchess laughed. "Eleanor, Carlisle is a Duke and a peer of the realm. The Ton would not dare to disparage him. He is a wealthy and powerful man who can do as he chooses. If he wants to marry you, no one can gainsay him."

"But that's it, he doesn't want to marry me. He's being forced into it. I can't let him have no choice in the matter."

The Duchess sat back and studied Eleanor. "Eleanor, why do you think Carlisle wouldn't rejoice at this situation?"

"Well, I think I've said."

"No, you've said why you are not pleased with it, and *you've* said why *you* think he might be unhappy, but you haven't heard *his* opinion yet."

Eleanor bit her lip, uneasy with what the Duchess was telling her, but not knowing how to rebut her politely. She was a Duchess after all, and now it looked like she might be her mother-in-law. Eleanor didn't know how to admit the worry she was feeling. She knew the nobility viewed marriage as a business arrangement, but she wanted a husband whom she could love and who loved her in return. A forced marriage was not the path to romance.

The Duchess eyed her cautiously. Eleanor hadn't answered her last comment, so now she tried for diplomacy. "Perhaps it's best if the Duke can weigh in on the matter himself."

"I'm sure he will," the Duchess replied dryly, "once he's feeling better. I should see what the doctor has to say, and you should go to your room and try to get more sleep as I'm sure you didn't get much rest last night while you were tending to my son."

Eleanor felt weary though her brain was moving in all directions at once so she didn't suppose that she would fall back asleep. Still, she nodded and arose with the Duchess. Jamie's mother came over and embraced Eleanor in a cloud of lavender and warmth. The Duchess really was a lovely woman, but Eleanor wondered if her marriage was arranged or had she been in love with Jamie's father?

The Duchess walked back through the connecting door to check on her son, and Eleanor thought about following her. She wanted to know how he was feeling this morning, but she was not ready to face him yet or to hear anymore lecturing from Mr. Stimpson, so she dragged herself to the corridor and down to her own room.

She was still wearing the dress she had put on yesterday though it was wrinkled from sleeping in it all night. How could she have fallen asleep? Eleanor had only meant to sit with Jamie to monitor his night and then slip out early before anyone else woke. It had been a dreadful mistake to lie down next to him, but a delicious one, she had to admit. He'd been a warm male wrapping her in his scent and comfort.

There were two letters propped on the stand next to her bed. Eleanor sat and opened them, hoping that one was an offer of a position. She could pack and go before anyone realized if she had a place, but it turned out both posts were filled long before. One problem in living so far from London was that the newspapers didn't reach Devon for days, and anything printed in them was old news, to say nothing of the time it took for a response to arrive at the intended employer.

Eleanor sighed. There was just one position left of the three she had applied for, but she didn't know when or if she would hear back from it. Perhaps she should just pack her bags and leave. If she were in London, she would have a better chance to find an open job for a governess. But reaching London would expend the last of her monies, and she would have nothing to live on if it took a while to find a position.

She loosened her dress and let it fall to the floor. It was such a wrinkled mess it didn't matter, and she was too tired to care. In her chemise, Eleanor climbed into her bed and drifted away with vivid dreams of appearing in a London ballroom on Jamie's arm where her clothes disappeared, and all the Ton pointed and laughed at her. When she looked at Jamie, he turned away, his face stern and implacable, while she cried and tried to cover herself.

Chapter Fourteen

Jamie was going mad. He hadn't seen Eleanor for two long days. Bates, Stimpson, and his mother were conspiring to keep him in bed, and Eleanor had not visited the sickroom once. His mother assured him that Eleanor was all right, but busy with other matters. Jamie feared what those other matters might be. Suppose she was planning to flee the house. Would anyone else stop her?

He was feeling much better, and he determined to get up and search the house until he found her. His mother had explained how they'd discovered him with Eleanor in his bed. Jamie told her the truth: he asked for comfort in his delirium and Eleanor had complied, but nothing untoward had occurred. The Duchess agreed, but both knew the consequences of the incident.

Jamie was perfectly fine with those results. Marriage to Eleanor was what he wanted, and the circumstances didn't bother him if he accomplished his goal. But he thought Eleanor was upset after her voiced anxieties about him being compromised into marriage and each hour that passed without her appearance only solidified Jamie's own worries about her state of mind.

The minute Bates had passed out of the room with the remains of his breakfast tray, Jamie was out of his bed. He held onto the bedpost until a momentary wooziness passed, then proceeded to his wardrobe and dressed. He wasn't feeling as steady as he imagined, but he determined to find Eleanor and speak to her.

Jamie couldn't do much about the fine reddish stubble that covered his cheeks. Bates was to return with hot water to shave him, but if Jamie waited, they would put back in bed, and he'd lose his chance to escape. He cleaned his teeth and give his face a quick scrubbing, then ran his fingers through his hair to arrange it into some order. Jamie didn't look his usual self, but it would have to do for the time being. It was more important that he find his wife-to-be and reassure her he would do the right thing by her.

He peeked out into the hallway outside his bedroom suite to find it empty. Eleanor would not be in her own room at this hour. He had discovered that she was an early riser. Jamie was also sure she would not have gone riding. While she had found a latent fondness for the exercise, Eleanor was not confident enough to ride without him at her side — at least, he hoped so.

His mother would not be up yet so Eleanor would not be with her. The Duchess preferred to rise later and take a breakfast tray in her room. Once she rose and dressed, though, she would check on his progress, and she would raise the alarm if Bates hadn't already discovered Jamie out of bed and peached on him. They were treating him like a six-year-old boy, Jamie thought with a snort.

Eleanor would either be walking in the gardens or in the library or office, he decided. It pleased Jamie that he knew her schedule so well. His Eleanor was an orderly creature, one of the many things he liked about her.

He strode briskly but quietly to the stairs. Halfway down, Jamie realized that Robert was staring up at him. He raised a finger to his lips, signaling silence, and Robert nodded. Inwardly, Jamie thought he wasn't behaving much better than the six-year-old he had earlier disparaged, but a man must do what a man found necessary.

Jamie tried the library first, but it was empty. He was sure that Eleanor must be out in the gardens but checked the office first just in case. Jamie was feeling stronger, the more he moved about, but he was very much afraid that it was a temporary situation.

He was in luck. Eleanor's head was bent over something she was writing. She sat in his usual chair, and Jamie savored the sight of her. She must have sensed him and lifted her face toward the door. He saw joy, dread, panic, and something else pass over her face in an instant, and his stomach sank. Still, Jamie was a brave man, and he entered the room and took a seat across the desk from Eleanor.

"Miss Mortimer, Eleanor, surely you are not working on my correspondence?" he asked in an attempt to lighten the mood. Eleanor bit her lip and nodded nervously.

"Yes, Your Grace, with the help of your mother. She has given me some direction, and I learned some of your habits before your illness." Eleanor attempted a smile, but it fell flat.

Something was seriously wrong with Eleanor. Jamie had expected some trepidation and doubt, but she was far more upset than Jamie had thought she might be. He *knew* allowing two days to go by without talking to her was a mistake.

"Your Grace, Eleanor?" Jamie teased. He wanted to go to her and pull her out of that chair into his arms, but it was best that the desk remained between them for now. "I thought I was Jamie now."

She glanced at the doorway as if she thought to make a run for it, but Jamie was between her and the door. Eleanor sighed. "Jamie."

Jamie found he was leaning forward as if his body had a magnet and she was made of iron, so he forced himself to sit back. He did not want to spook her.

"Eleanor, we need to talk."

She stiffened. Jamie didn't think her back could get any straighter, but she didn't answer him, so he went on.

"First, I want to apologize for the other night. The incident was entirely my fault." He studied her face, but Eleanor appeared to be looking right past him. "In my delirium, I did not behave as a gentleman should. If I had been well, I would never have asked you to stay with me — like that." Jamie could feel the sweat causing his shirt to cling to his back, but he knew he no longer had a fever. It was merely nerves.

Eleanor's eyes snapped back to his face with a touch of anger and dismay showing in her expression. Her lower lip trembled, but still, she did not answer him, so Jamie continued grimly.

"Therefore, due to the assembly who charged into my room without warning, we must enter into marriage."

Eleanor's eyes frosted over, and Jamie realized he was bungling this proposal. Perhaps he should have waited until he was feeling a little better because he couldn't seem to get his wits about him.

"Thank you for the kind offer, Your Grace, but an offer of marriage is unnecessary, gracious as the message was. You may free your mind on that score."

Jamie felt his temper rise. Eleanor was acting the ice queen, so perhaps a little fire would melt that reserve.

"Indeed, madam," he answered in his most ducal manner. "It was not an offer. We will marry, Eleanor. My honor requires it and your own."

He was spoiling for a fight. Turned down for marriage twice before, Jamie reacted with shock the first time and equanimity the second, but he would not allow Eleanor to refuse him. Not because he couldn't take a refusal, but because he wouldn't take one from her. They were meant to be together. He was sure of it. He loved her, and he thought she loved him. At the least, he attracted her physically, and he could build on that.

But Jamie wasn't prepared for it when Eleanor burst into tears.

ELEANOR KNEW SHE WAS running out of time. The Duchess gave her reports on Jamie's recovery. He was improving daily and complaining vociferously about having to stay in bed. She had scanned the latest newspaper to arrive and responded to the one advertisement for a governess position. Still, she didn't have much hope of hearing back in enough time.

The Duchess had used her contacts to send for a special license. It would arrive within the week, Eleanor guessed, as the Duchess continued to make plans for a small wedding feast. Presumably, she was consulting with her son, but Eleanor was banned from his chamber now that the damage was done.

Jamie's mother had been in a suspiciously cheerful mood the last few days. If Eleanor didn't know Jamie had not fallen ill on purpose, she would have thought the Duchess had planned the whole affair. Though she couldn't fathom why the Duchess would want a vicar's daughter for her son's wife.

Eleanor herself alternated between despair and hope. She was dreadfully in love with Jamie. She could admit to herself that she had wanted to marry him, but the method in which the events had occurred left her cold and worried about the future. These feelings only grew as the days passed until her nerves were as taut as a bowstring.

Jamie's appearance at the office door left Eleanor muddled. Poor Jamie looked pale and unshaven, so unlike his usual immaculate person. His cravat was tied untidily, and his hair stood straight up in the air. She wanted to soothe and comfort him, but that was how she got into this mess in the first place. So Eleanor straightened her shoulders and set to doing her best to refuse the offer of marriage she knew was coming.

She was as surprised as Jamie when she burst into tears.

He was around the desk and had lifted her into his arms before she could look for a handkerchief. Jamie sat in the now vacant chair with Eleanor in his lap and let her cry all over his messy cravat. He rubbed circles on her back and nestled her head under his chin as if she were a small child again crying for her mother.

When she had ceased, Jamie whipped off his cravat and let her wipe her face and blow her nose in a most disorderly and unladylike manner.

It would have mortified Eleanor if she wasn't so exhausted from the fit of tears. She had not been sleeping well, too worried for restful slumber.

"There, there, sweetheart," Jamie crooned. "Feeling better?"

Eleanor nodded, her face blotchy and red. *If that doesn't scare him off, I don't know what will,* she thought.

"Eleanor," he said. "I know that I didn't ask you correctly. I'm nervous, to tell the truth, and I botched it badly. But despite all, will you marry me?"

"Jamie, I can't," she answered as she felt his body tense. But he didn't show his temper again.

Instead, he asked gently, "Can you explain your refusal to me? Because I must confess, I think we should get along just fine. I would be proud to have you as my Duchess."

Eleanor faltered. She didn't have the words to explain that she didn't care about any of that, well, not much. It was that she wanted him to love her as she loved him. Eleanor fidgeted with the rumpled cravat in her hands and sighed.

"I don't know, Jamie. I understand how this might look, but we are so far away from society I think any gossip might blow over. So, I will find a governess position, and you can forget this ever occurred." Eleanor peeked up at Jamie's impassive face.

"Perhaps I can persuade you otherwise," he whispered, and he tipped her face up to his. His lips came down on hers, firm and tender, molding to her mouth and sending sparks throughout Eleanor's body.

Despite her best efforts, Eleanor's body strained to his, and he pulled her closer. Her position on his lap left her in no doubt that Jamie wanted her. His tongue pushed at her lips and slipped inside her mouth to tangle with her own tongue in a sinuous dance.

They kissed what seemed to be hours, and Eleanor felt bereft when Jamie withdrew, pulling his head back and leaning his forehead against hers as he struggled for breath.

"Marry me, Eleanor," Jamie asked, his voice husky with his passion.

She closed her eyes and said, "Yes."

Chapter Fifteen

The wait seemed interminable to Jamie. It was another five days before the courier came with the special license for him to wed Eleanor. He had left her in the office flushed and shy once he had gotten her agreement and gone back to his bed where he collapsed for the next day. His mother and Bates had scolded him, but Jamie could tell they were both pleased when he announced his forthcoming marriage.

Everyone but Eleanor knew he would marry her anyway, but Jamie relished the formality of his engagement, short as it might end up being. They allowed Eleanor back into his bedroom for prescribed times to read to him, but only for short periods. She was quiet otherwise, and Jamie worried about that, but once he had her as a wife and away from all the other eyes, he could straighten out whatever matters were bothering her. Until then, he tried to spend as much time with her as allowed.

They kept a strict eye on the two of them which Jamie found somewhat ridiculous. Much freedom was allowed to them earlier, but now nothing would do, but they must have a groom ride out with them on their morning rides. Mr. Stimpson took Eleanor's place in his office, a much less desirable prospect for Jamie. He enjoyed the hours he had spent in companionship with Eleanor. She was a hard worker but intelligent, and they had passed hours away in conversation as they worked on his correspondence. Mr. Stimpson was a genial sort, now he wasn't competing for Eleanor's hand, but by no means provided the entertainment that Eleanor could for him by being in the room.

Jamie was lovesick. He had never felt like this before. In some ways, these feelings belied his dignity, but he didn't care. The thought of having Eleanor to call his own made him giddy.

Meanwhile, his betrothed didn't speak much, no matter how he tried to entice her. Teasing didn't work, only a small smile for his best efforts. Eleanor didn't look unhappy, but neither was she the blushing bride. She seemed more... resigned.

Still, Jamie was confident that all would be well once she was over her nerves. The circumstances of the betrothal and mourning for her father meant that the wedding would be small. Mr. Stimpson would marry them in the front sitting room with his mother, Bates, and Mrs. Makepeace as witnesses.

Jamie paced as he waited for his mother and the bride to arrive. The others were already there, Mrs. Makepeace, her manner aflutter, and Mr. Stimpson, solemnly dressed in his best clothes. Bates was himself, silent and attentive as always.

Stimpson would stay on at Wykeham Hall until the repairs to the manse were complete. The man seemed to adjust well to his new role and had already paid another visit on his own to the Beaton household, much to Jamie's satisfaction. He bore the Beaton's no ill-will and thought Miss Beaton would make a very satisfactory wife for the vicar.

Jamie intended to remove to London with his bride and his mother after the ceremony. The trip would take several days, but they would make it a leisurely journey. In some ways, he wished his mother would not be with them, but she had no other company to make the return trip. She had put all her own business aside to make the journey to Devon for him. Still, his mind thought of ways he and Eleanor could have taken advantage of the closed coach if they were traveling alone.

He pulled at the lace edging on his sleeve and looked once more to the doorway. He couldn't help but be nervous. Surely all bridegrooms were nervous on their wedding day. Once Eleanor appeared Jamie knew his anxiety would settle. He still feared that she would disappear before the ceremony, off to be a governess and leaving him bereft.

There was a noise from the corridor, and the Duchess entered the room, her silk gown rustling. She gave her son a bright smile and a kiss on the cheek and then patted his chest.

"Mama," Jamie returned the smile. For so long it had been just the two of them, and now it would be three. God willing, more as time went by.

"Eleanor will be right along," she whispered. "Be good to her, James. She's very nervous."

Jamie tensed, but he didn't answer because Eleanor glided into the room. She dressed in the dark blue dress he had bought for her in Okehampton, a concession to her state of mourning for her bridal ceremony. Her dark hair was up in curls, and someone had placed small pearls among the tendrils that shone against the brown gloss of her tresses.

He regretted now he hadn't sent to London for some of the jewels that would soon belong to her as the new Duchess of Carlisle. It hadn't seemed worth it though Jamie had asked her, and she concurred with him. His mother had also offered to lend her a necklace, but Eleanor refused. She wore the locket that had belonged to her mother which she insisted was what her parents would have liked for her wedding day.

Her face was pale, but her eyes fixed on him, steady and warm, and Jamie let out a breath he didn't know he was holding inside. He walked forward to meet her, and Eleanor gave him a tremulous smile. Jamie lifted her hand and bestowed a kiss on the smooth skin.

Jamie led her to stand in front of Mr. Stimpson. The vicar conducted the service, and Jamie knew he responded appropriately, but he scarce knew the words being said. When the time came, he put the plain gold band on her finger. Jamie had sent to Okehampton for the ring. He told Eleanor he would give her a better one when they reached London, but she didn't care. Eleanor might cherish the simple gold ring, but Jamie would shower her with jewels from the Ducal coffers once she was his Duchess.

The ceremony was over, and Jamie carefully placed a quick kiss on Eleanor's lips. Her lower lip was trembling, he hoped from emotion and not fear.

Mrs. Makepeace had organized a grand wedding breakfast, far too elaborate for the few people who partook. Eleanor had insisted that both Bates and Mrs. Makepeace, in their capacity as witnesses, sit with them to eat.

Jamie sat Eleanor at his right while his mother took the seat to his left. He leaned toward her once he was in his chair and observed, "Well, Duchess, our first meal together as man and wife." It pleased him to see her cheeks bloom with color.

Eleanor pursed her lips together. "What am I to call you now?" Jamie winked at her, and she added, "In public, sir."

He laughed, but his mother answered for him. "Duke or Carlisle will do." She frowned mockingly at Jamie, but her eyes sparkled. Jamie could feel his mother's happiness warm him. His choice of bride pleased her well.

His new wife, however, was a different story. Eleanor lapsed back to quiet. Generally, Jamie didn't mind that. He was not garrulous, and Eleanor's usual rectitude suited him. Today, however, he wanted her to be happy and to display it in her speech and manner. Jamie ignored the small niggle of unease that went through him at Eleanor's somber face. All would be well once some time had passed, and she settled into her new role.

His Eleanor was a passionate woman. Her kisses had fired his blood, and he shifted uneasily at the thought of her naked in his bed. He thought tonight would never arrive. Besides his own gratification, Jamie thought sharing a bed would go a long way to easing Eleanor's fears about his feelings toward her.

Eleanor didn't eat much, but then neither did Jamie. All too soon they finished the meal, and the three travelers bade their goodbyes. Jamie had still not discovered the discrepancy in the Hall's books, but he had the older ones packed away to take back to London where he could study them at his leisure. He was sure once he concentrated, he'd discover what the old Baron had been up to and be able to balance the accounts.

The two coaches drew up in the front drive. Bates and the Duchess's maid were riding in her coach and Eleanor, Jamie, and his mother would take his. They'd tied Ajax to the back, unhappy at his circumstances. Jamie would ride him later in the day, but for the nonce, he intended to attend his new bride.

He helped his mother and Eleanor into the carriage, then entered and sat across from them. Both women were conversing pleasantly about the trip and London. The furthest that Eleanor had ever been from Sourton she could remember was a short trip to Exeter. Her parents had come to Devon when she was a baby from the Oxford area, but she had been far too young to remember anything from that time.

Jamie settled back in his seat, content for the first time in a long while. His wife — *his wife*! — looked up at him with a smile. Eleanor seemed to be also relaxing. He would be proud to have her on his arm at assemblies and balls, to sit across from her at meals, and to share her bed. The thought made him shift again, and he looked out the window, attempting to take his mind off the coming evening; otherwise, this carriage ride could become exceedingly painful.

The three conversed at first, and then the Dowager Duchess pulled a book out of her reticule which she perused until her head nodded and she fell asleep, her head forward on her chest.

"Duchess," Jamie whispered. Eleanor glanced at him, but she didn't respond to her new title. "Eleanor, I mean *you*."

"Oh," she said. "I didn't... I mean..." She was flustered, and Jamie grinned, happy to have discombobulated her a little out of her subdued mood.

She rolled her eyes. "I'm not sure I'll ever become accustomed to that title. The only Duchess I've ever met is your mother."

"And now yourself," Jamie reminded her. He leaned forward and took her gloved hands into his own. "You will meet other Duchesses and Countesses and others of the Ton in London. You must remember that you are just as entitled as any of them except the Royal Dukes and Duchesses, and you are of higher stature than most. Yet all of those women put their shoes and hats on the same as you."

Eleanor laughed, a musical sound that filled Jamie's chest with warmth. "This is my only hat at present, sir. I expect most of those women have a different hat to wear for every occasion."

"When we get to London, Mama will take you shopping, and you must buy everything you might want or need. Cost is not an object, and I expect my Duchess to have at least twenty hats in her wardrobe."

"Goodness, I will have to take over another room for my clothing at that rate." Eleanor gave Jamie a look that said she thought him too extravagant, but she would discover how lavish he could be. Jamie looked forward to spoiling his new wife once they reached Town.

Eleanor smiled and then looked out the carriage window. Jamie frowned as he watched her fingers nervously entwine, a habit Eleanor had that she displayed when upset. Her face was serene though, so he forwent asking her about it.

"Soon we will reach an inn where we can stop for luncheon. It is a pleasant place. I stopped there on my way to Sourton and found the food tasty." Eleanor nodded, so Jamie continued. "You must be hungry. You didn't eat much at breakfast."

"Nerves, I suppose. You must also be ready to eat something. Your appetite seems to have returned since your illness." Her fingers stilled, and Jamie relaxed slightly.

"Eleanor, I want you to know..." The carriage slowing interrupted Jamie, and his mother stirred, woken by the change in speed. They were turning into the yard of the inn he had just mentioned, and his chance was lost—for now.

Chapter Sixteen

They traveled late to reach the inn where Jamie planned to stay for the night. A broken wheel on the Duchess's coach had delayed them though it only took an hour for someone to make repairs. After lunch, much to Eleanor's relief, Jamie had ridden Ajax, leaving her alone in the carriage with his mother. The Dowager Duchess was an enjoyable traveling companion, talking about Jamie's childhood and tutoring Eleanor on what she should expect when they reached London.

Jamie ate well at luncheon, back to his usual appetite, but Eleanor had merely nibbled, her stomach too upset from anxiety. She had calmed during the afternoon with Jamie out of the carriage to remind her of her married state and what it portended. Eleanor was torn. She rejoiced in her marriage to Jamie, but she longed to be sure of his regard for her. Jamie treated her kindly as she imagined he would, no matter who his wife was. However, she wanted more than kindness from him.

There was one uneasy moment with the Duchess late in the afternoon. Jamie's mother had taken her hand, for the first time since Eleanor had known her, her composure missing.

"My dear," she began. "Your mother passed away some time ago, and I'm not sure if any other maternal figure existed in your life."

At Eleanor's bewildered headshake, the Duchess went on. "Do you know what happens between a man and his wife on their wedding night?"

Eleanor's face turned red, her neck hot, as the import of the Duchess's words sank in. Eleanor was a country girl, and she had helped deliver babies, so she had some idea. She had felt the evidence of Jamie's desire for her when he kissed her. She was a little confused about the actual mechanics, to be honest, but it would horrify her to hear the details from Jamie's mother.

"I believe so, Your Grace," she muttered, her eyes fixed on her hands in her lap.

"Do you have questions, Eleanor?"

"No, none, thank you." Eleanor just wanted this conversation over and done with. Any hope of enjoying her dinner disappeared along with the fading light of day. She squeezed her hands together as the Duchess gave her a searching look, but changed the conversation to a charity she contributed to in town she thought Eleanor might wish to sponsor. It provided a home for orphaned girls and taught them employment in the millinery trade.

Eleanor nodded her head at appropriate intervals and her embarrassment faded. She enjoyed Jamie's kisses, and she would do her duty as a wife, but the little she had learned of the marriage bed told her that husbands and wives shared it only to procreate. The little she knew of the nobility indicated that they were even worse. The husband would get his heir and spare on his wife, then never bother her again, preferring to lie with a mistress. Mrs. Makepeace had been quite voluble on the subject.

It was bad enough that her new husband did not love her. Eleanor would not even have the chance to win his regard as husbands and wives in the Ton did not spend much time together. Her stomach roiled, and she let out a sigh.

They arrived at the inn where they to spend the night at dusk. The innkeeper led Eleanor to a large chamber in the back where it was quiet. She could wash before going down to dinner. The Duchess was in the room next to hers. She wasn't sure where Jamie's room was. He had helped them down from the carriage and then gone off to see to Ajax's care, letting the innkeeper lead them upstairs.

There was a knock at the door. Eleanor supposed that someone was bringing up her bags, or a maid had come looking for her, and she opened the door to find her new husband standing there.

"Oh, I thought you were the innkeeper." She sounded inane.

Jamie gave her a crooked grin. "No, just your husband. May I enter?"

"Of course," Eleanor said and backed up to give him room. She waited, supposing he had come to escort her back downstairs to the private parlor he had secured for their dining.

"This is a nice chamber, comfortable and quiet."

"Yes," Eleanor agreed. "Very pleasant. I hope that your room is as agreeable."

"Eleanor?" Jamie tilted his head and studied her. "We are to share a room." His face changed, became sterner. "Unless you'd rather I found my own chamber."

Her face hot, Eleanor acknowledged her gaffe. "No, no, I didn't realize. I'm not used, you see..."

Jamie relaxed and took her hands. "This is new for both of us, but I am confident we will find our way. Tonight of all nights we will share a bed, for it is our wedding night. I want my wife curled around me as we sleep together."

Eleanor blushed, but the idea of sleeping in Jamie's arms warmed her heart. She managed a nod, and Jamie dropped his arms. "Have you left any water for me? I need to wash the dust of the road and the smell of my horse off before we dine."

She indicated the privacy screen, and Jamie went behind it. Eleanor could hear water being poured and she marveled at the idea she was now privy to her husband's more intimate moments.

Jamie called to her from behind the screen. "I have ordered a bath for you here after dinner. I thought you might enjoy a nice soak before bed."

"Thank you, I would," Eleanor answered. "But what..."

Jamie laughed. "I am to have my bath in another chamber. The innkeeper has arranged it so you may have privacy and relax."

Eleanor nodded and realized that Jamie could not see her. "Of course. My thanks again."

Jamie came out from behind the screen, his face still gleaming from his scrubbing. "Eleanor, it is my privilege to care for your needs. You don't have to keep thanking me, my dear."

Suddenly shy, Eleanor just shrugged. "We should go down to our dinner. I don't want the Duchess to wait for us."

"My mother will dine in her own chamber tonight and won't be joining us. While she assured me she was tired, I suspect she aims to give us some privacy in our meal. We have had little chance to speak together since the wedding ceremony, or truth to tell, even much in the days before it."

Jamie's stomach growled at that moment, and he looked nonplussed, but Eleanor giggled. Her husband did like to eat. "Come, madam. The dinner bell has rung," he said with a grin, and Eleanor laughed again. Maybe the two of them could make a go of this marriage anyway, forced or not.

CARRYING HIS SHOES, Jamie crept along the corridor back to his bedroom. He wore his shirt loose and just his breeches, sure he would not run into anyone on the way at this late hour. Their dinner had run late, but though his body wanted to sweep Eleanor up and carry her to their bed, his mind and heart knew she needed the respite. His mother had had a quiet word with him earlier, and while he was sure Eleanor was a maiden, his mother confirmed that he needed to take his time with her. A few glasses of wine with dinner had relaxed her more. The bath he had arranged should have eased her even more; he felt better after his own hot soak.

When he reached his door, he stopped, uncertain whether he could just walk in or whether he should knock first. Jamie didn't want to startle Eleanor, so he tapped on the door. He heard a sound and turned the doorknob.

Eleanor was standing by the window clad in a simple white nightdress. Her brown hair was loose, down around her shoulders in a chestnut stream that made her look young and very lovely. The tub had been removed, but a servant had started a fire that warmed the room. The heat added additional color to Eleanor's cheeks, or perhaps it was just maidenly thoughts of what was to come.

"Hello," Jamie said. He felt blood rush to his own face at the banality of his greeting. He walked over and placed his shoes on the floor near the wardrobe. Bates could look for them in the morning — hopefully, late in the morning. Jamie was expecting a delayed start to their journey the next day if his night went the way he hoped.

"Hello," Eleanor answered, a tiny smile flashing across her face only to disappear again. She crossed her arms over her chest to cover herself, and Jamie loved her for her modesty and shyness. God willing, she would become accustomed to his presence in her bedchamber. Jamie was not one of those who believed husband and wife should each have their own room. He intended to share a bed with his wife for every night she would allow it.

Eleanor walked to the bed, and Jamie watched her square her shoulders and take a deep breath as she climbed in.

"Eleanor, wait."

She froze and then turned to look over her shoulder at him.

"I thought perhaps we could sit by the fire for a little while, relax with each other. Today has been a rush, and there is no hurry to go to bed unless you're very fatigued."

Eleanor complied, coming over to take a chair in front of the fireplace, but she cast him a suspicious look as she passed. She was no fool, his new wife, and Jamie knew she suspected him of prevarication.

To be honest, Jamie was near driven mad by the glimpses of her body afforded by the sheer nightclothes. Eleanor's dainty white foot dangled from the chair carelessly, the other tucked under her rump. Her breasts strained against the linen of her nightgown as she absently pulled up a shoulder strap from the loose top. She was utterly seductive and not even conscious of her allure.

She folded her hands in her lap and waited for Jamie to say something more, but he was lost, trying to control his errant body that didn't want to talk, but wanted to seize, to caress, and love his wife.

"Would you like something to drink, perhaps?" He spied a decanter and some glasses. Jamie was not a big drinker, but a drink before bed seemed like a good idea right now.

Eleanor bit her lip and nodded. "I believe so, just a little, though, for me."

Jamie poured their drinks, his considerably larger and passed a glass to Eleanor. She sipped cautiously and made a face. Jamie laughed.

"Is that your first brandy?" he asked.

"Aye," she admitted. "It makes my nose tickle." She put her glass aside and smiled at him, a real smile, and something clenched tightly inside Jamie relaxed.

He leaned forward and asked, "How are you, Eleanor? Tell me truly."

Eleanor didn't flinch but considered his question before she answered. "It's strange, Jamie, all of this—to me." She gestured around the room with her hand. "Not just the Duchess part. I'm sure that will take me some time to get used to if I ever do, but being here with you in dishabille."

Jamie concentrated on her words. She was so brave, his new wife, and he would do his best to make her proud of him and to not hurt her. He waited for her to finish her speech.

"I realize that there are different sorts of marriages. My parents shared a room, but I understand that most of the Ton are more...

formal, I guess you would say. A husband and a wife have separate rooms and separate lives."

"I do not know how we will go on," she finished, speaking with just the slightest quiver in her voice.

Jamie put down his glass and rose, only to fall to his knees before Eleanor. He took her hands into his as he answered her.

"A Duke's life is full of formalities, but I pledge this to you, Eleanor. We will share a room and a bed and our lives as much as you wish. That is the kind of marriage I wish, and I hope you want that, too."

He leaned forward and met her lips with his own. Eleanor responded eagerly, and their passion took hold as it had each time they kissed. Jamie broke the kiss and arose, then lifted Eleanor into his arms and carried her to bed.

Chapter Seventeen

The trip lasted several more days as the bridal couple was in no hurry to end their journey. The Dowager Duchess delighted to see her son's joy in his new bride, and the thought their marital activities could result in grandchildren all the sooner only enhanced her willingness to tarry. Jamie often rode in the coach with them, pointing out passing attractions to Eleanor to whom these were all new sights.

They came within the city limits of London, and Eleanor amused and entertained Jamie with her observations and amazement at the numerous buildings and crowds of people. She didn't like the putrid smells or the smoggy air that Londoners were used to as one got closer to the center of the city, but Jamie admired that as a measure of her common sense.

Finally, the coachman pulled the carriage up in front of a spacious mansion. Eleanor stared wide-eyed as Jamie smiled. "Welcome to Carlisle House," he said.

A bewildering and seemingly vast amount of servants awaited them inside in the front hallway. Eleanor counted at least five footmen, more maids than she had ever seen, and various other workers whose positions she couldn't fathom. The housekeeper, a very prim woman named Mrs. Fellowes, introduced Eleanor to each person though she knew she would never remember all the various names and titles. She assigned a pleasant young girl named Martin to Eleanor as her ladies maid until she decided on a permanent person in the position as Mrs. Fellowes informed her to Martin's clear dismay. It took Eleanor a moment to realize that Martin was the girl's last name; apparently, it had been unsuitable to call Anna back at Wykeham Hall by her first name.

Jamie and the Dowager stayed by her side during the introductions, then Jamie escorted her to her new chambers. A lovely blue and gilt sitting room led to a similarly decorated bedchamber beyond. Jamie had sent word ahead of the new Duchess, and they had moved the Dowager's things to a different suite, much to Eleanor's dismay. However, her new mother-in-law informed her it was proper for the change to take place, and it should not concern Eleanor.

Jamie had left her at the door, and Eleanor stood in the room's center while Martin bustled about trying to impress her with her efficiency in putting away Eleanor's few bits of clothing. She was a quiet little thing, but Eleanor wasn't used to having another person fluttering about her. Still, Martin was trying very hard to be considered for the position. Eleanor supposed that if she had to have a personal maid, then Martin would do as well as any.

"Your Grace, would you like me to loosen your gown? I thought you might rest for a while before dinner."

Eleanor considered the idea, but she was restless after sitting in the carriage for so long. "I think I'd like to find the Duke," she said.

Martin curtsied. "Let me find a footman to take you to him."

Eleanor almost rebelled, but then realized that she wouldn't be able to find Jamie in this vast house. Until she learned her way around, she was at the mercy of the servants.

"Thank you, Martin," she sighed. "That would be perfect."

She followed the tall liveried footman down the stairs and through a mystifying maze of hallways. The servant left her at the door to Jamie's study where he was working at an impressive mahogany desk, sorting through papers with the aid of a young man. He looked up as Eleanor tapped on the door, and both men rose from their chairs.

"My dear, come in. This is my secretary, Mr. Phillips. John, I'd like to introduce you to my wife, the new Duchess of Carlisle." The young man bowed, a broad smile on his face. Eleanor liked him immediately. He seemed a friendly, useful sort, and Jamie had often spoken of him and his efficiency as they worked on his correspondence to London.

"Mr. Phillips, it is lovely to meet you at last. The Duke often spoke of your competence and skill."

Mr. Phillips blushed, which made him look even younger. He stood with his hands folded in front of him, the tips of his ears red, betraying his self-consciousness.

"Can I help you with something, Duchess" Jamie sounded a bit distracted, and he kept glancing down at the papers on his desk. "Are your rooms satisfactory?"

"Yes, they are lovely. I wondered if you needed my help with anything." Eleanor gave him a tentative smile, but Jamie had picked up a paper and was looking at it.

"Thank you, my dear, but I believe John has matters well under control. We'll just go over a few items, and I will see you at dinner."

Mr. Phillips gave her a sympathetic smile, but Eleanor's heart sank. She had no idea what to do with herself, but the hope that Jamie would ease her way into her new surroundings seemed more likely to be unfulfilled than not. She nodded and left the room, her departure unnoticed by her new husband.

Eleanor wandered down the corridor. All around her servants were busy, but their Duchess was at a loss as to what to do with herself. Perhaps she should find her way back to her rooms. She could read or write a letter, except Eleanor didn't know where the library was to select a book and she had no one to write a letter to.

It was humiliating, but she finally stopped a footman and had him guide her to the library in the house. It was a large room with shelf upon shelf of books of all types. They were ordered neatly, and Eleanor had no trouble finding the novels and making a selection. She was finished with Mr. Scott's works for the time being, but there were plenty of other authors to choose from. Jamie had not lied when he said the library at Carlisle House was well-stocked.

Then she needed to ask another footman to guide her back to her chambers. Eleanor heaved a sigh of relief when she reached her sitting room but found Martin sitting in the corner of her bedroom, mending one of Eleanor's older chemises. She jumped up when Eleanor entered the room.

"So sorry, Your Grace. I thought I'd work on your wardrobe a bit while you were gone."

Embarrassed that the maid found her clothing wanting, Eleanor was still honest enough to admit that Martin was not at fault. Her clothes were not up to par for a Duchess. The Dowager had promised to take her shopping soon, and while Eleanor was still not out of mourning, she needed to replace what wasn't up to London standards.

"That's fine, Martin. I'll sit out here and read for a while." She backed out of the bedroom and took a seat on the lovely blue velvet sofa in her sitting room. Eleanor slipped her shoes off and pulled her legs up beneath her and opened her book.

When Martin came out to ready her for dinner, Eleanor was napping, her book fallen to the floor. The maid exclaimed over her awkward position, saying that Eleanor should have used the bed, but Eleanor waved off her concerns. The maid had laid out the dark blue dress that Eleanor had been married in for her to wear to dinner and Eleanor gently touched the sleeve, remembering that day, not a week past.

She felt much recovered after her nap. Of course, Jamie had to see to his correspondence and business. After his long absence, there must be much work to catch up on despite his efforts at Wykeham Hall, and Jamie was a conscientious man. Look at the efforts he made at Wykeham Hall.

Eleanor made it down the stairs where a footman was waiting to direct her to the room where the Dowager was waiting for her and her son. Jamie had not yet arrived, and Eleanor wondered if she should go back upstairs to find him, but she sat down next to her mother-in-law when the older woman motioned for her to join her.

The Dowager Duchess was very gracious and kind to Eleanor. She must have sensed Eleanor's sense of misplacement and arranged that they would go shopping the very next day. Once Eleanor had some suitable clothes, the Dowager would take her out to meet people, a prospect that Eleanor dreaded, but which seemed unavoidable in the circumstances. She agreed and tried to look enthusiastic about the undertaking.

Jamie arrived just as the gong sounded, looking dashing in his dinner clothes. He escorted his wife and mother into the dining room which dwarfed the one at Wykeham Hall. Eleanor couldn't imagine a dinner with enough people to fill the table, but the Dowager assured her that parties of that size were a regular occurrence, especially during the Season or when Parliament was in session.

The food was excellent, but the multiple courses for just the three of them seemed excessive to Eleanor. She thought the leftovers would feed several of the poor families back in Sourton, but chose not to remark on it. In fact, she didn't speak much at all during the meal, letting Jamie and his mother carry the conversation.

When dinner ended, Eleanor felt relieved. Now she would have some of Jamie's attention, and perhaps she could speak to him of some of her misgivings. But he soon dashed her hopes.

"I hope you will excuse me, my dear, but I fear I must return to Phillips, who has been laboring mightily while I dined with you. I'm sure you must be tired, though." He bent and kissed her forehead. "I'll be up later."

Eleanor nodded, trying to be forgiving, but the Dowager gave her a sharp look though she said nothing. Eleanor excused herself, pleading exhaustion, but the truth was that she didn't want to face the Dowager's pity any longer.

She found her way to her chamber where Martin was waiting to dress her in her nightclothes. Eleanor settled into bed with her book, but then curious climbed back out and wandered to the door that connected with Jamie's bedroom. It was unlocked, and she peeked in. Bates looked over from the wardrobe where he was pulling out the Duke's night robe.

"Can I help you, Your Grace?"

Eleanor stepped behind the door, conscious of her garb. "No, I wondered if His Grace had come up yet."

"Not yet, madam. I shall inform him you were looking for him when he arrives."

"Thank you, Bates, but that won't be necessary." Eleanor shut the door and rushed back to her bed. She settled back with her book, but she couldn't concentrate. She was anxious for Jamie to come to bed so she could speak to him. This wasn't quite how Eleanor had envisioned their married life after the bliss of the trip from Devon, though to be honest, it was only their first day in London.

She put the book aside, too restless to read, and waited for Jamie. In just the short time they had been married, Eleanor had grown used to sleeping with her husband. In this new bed and strange room, she longed for the comfort of his warm body next to hers.

Eleanor waited and waited. Twice she thought she heard a sound in the adjoining chamber and tiptoed to the doorway to listen, but Jamie still did not arrive. It was very late by the time he came to bed, and Eleanor had shed some tears. She pretended to be asleep when he pulled her next to him, but she lay with her eyes open for a long time after he blew out the candles.

Chapter Eighteen

When Eleanor awoke, Jamie was already gone. She touched his side of the bed, but it was cold so he must have been up for a while. There was a tap on the door, and Martin peeked her head into the room. Eleanor could not get used to the lack of privacy from the servants. She was unaccustomed to being dressed or undressed by another person and avoided it as much as she could to Martin's dismay. She knew the woman was doing her best to help Eleanor, and she would never take it out on Martin, but she felt stifled.

Martin was carrying a large tray. "The Duke thought you might like to take your breakfast in bed this morning."

Eleanor felt another niggle of discomfort at the idea that Jamie was trying to avoid her. "I can dress and take my breakfast with him downstairs," she said and got out of bed.

"Oh, no, Your Grace. The Duke was up early and has gone out riding. He said you weren't to be disturbed, that you had a restless night, and that I was to bring you your meal when it looked like you were stirring."

With no other choice, Eleanor climbed back into bed and waited for Martin to place the tray over her legs. She could not recall ever eating in bed before and found it somewhat awkward, even when Martin plumped up pillows behind her to help her sit up.

Once she finished, and Martin took away the tray, she allowed Eleanor up to dress her.

"You are going shopping with Her Grace today," Martin reminded her. "That is so exciting."

Apparently, her maid was looking forward to the day more than Eleanor was. The prospect of shopping for clothes was excruciating to her. On the other hand, she didn't have much of anything else to do. She could explore the house at her leisure, so the idea of getting out and having a look at the streets of London seemed a better choice. Eleanor had only caught glimpses through the windows of the coach yesterday.

Martin pulled one of her newer black dresses out of the wardrobe. Eleanor knew even though it was a new gown, it was still sadly lacking as far as the latest London fashions went. She could see that just by looking at the Dowager Duchess's apparel. She heaved a sigh but held out her arms for Martin to pull it over her head.

Once Eleanor was clothed, Martin had to do her hair. "Have you thought about having your hair cut, Your Grace? It is the latest fashion," she remarked as she brushed and pinned Eleanor's long hair. "I believe it would curl up prettily if you had it cut short."

"Perhaps," she answered. "I will have to ask the Duke which he prefers."

That must have been the correct answer because Martin smiled and patted the last curl in place. "Of course, you must do as your husband wishes."

Eleanor nodded absently. Martin had done something different with her hair, and it did look quite lovely. The arrangement made her thin face look fuller, prettier even. Topped with her new bonnet, she thought she'd do.

Feeling a little better, Eleanor descended the stairs to meet the Dowager.

"Your Grace," Eleanor said.

"My dear," her mother-in-law replied. "I hope you will allow me to call you Eleanor, and you should call me Elizabeth in private. We are family now, and all these rules may have a place, but not between us."

"Of course, Elizabeth. I would love that."

The Dowager Duchess swept through the open door and down the steps to the waiting carriage, Eleanor in her wake. The Duchess had her maid with her but had told Eleanor that one maid should be sufficient for today. Most of their purchases would be sent on later.

Elizabeth was as good as her word. She chatted easily with Eleanor, pointing out sights as they passed through the busy streets. They reached the shopping district all too soon and descended from the carriage onto the sidewalk. People were everywhere, window shopping, going in and out of shops. Eleanor had never seen so many stores. Okehampton was a mere village next to London.

She looked longingly into a bookstore as they passed by, but the Dowager said, "Not today, Eleanor. You may shop for books another time, but we have an appointment with my modiste, and we must not keep her waiting. Madame LeRoche is one of the finest dressmakers in London, and she has a long client list. She is taking you in hand as a special favor to me." The Dowager winked and added, "And because you are a Duchess and dressing you will be another feather in her cap."

Eleanor followed obediently, but her stomach was turning, and she was sorry now she had eaten that last scone. What if Madame LeRoche chose not to dress her once she saw her? Eleanor was not the typical English rose, being dark-haired and full in the bosom. Her worry was peaking when the Dowager turned into a tastefully decorated shop painted in green and gilt.

A voluble older woman dressed very modishly, a lacy white cap on her iron-gray hair greeted them. She grasped the Dowager's hand familiarly. "Your Grace, how lovely to see you. And with such news. A new daughter-in-law. So exciting, yes?"

Madame LeRoche had a slight accent, but whether real or feigned, Eleanor could not discern. Her own French was minimal, and she had not used it for a long while.

The modiste turned to her and gave Eleanor a long look, then walked around her in a circle while the Dowager stood to the side and waited. She stopped at Eleanor's front again, studying her figure while tapping a finger on her chin. Then Madame LeRoche reached forward and pulled at Eleanor's top, revealing more skin and the top of her chemise. Eleanor startled and then gasped as the dressmaker pinched her stays through the cloth of her dress.

Eleanor had thought Mrs. Glass, the dressmaker in Okehampton, to be forward, but she was nothing compared to Madame LeRoche. Her face was bright red with embarrassment, and she looked to the Dowager for aid, but her mother-in-law was nodding, her lips pursed as she studied the modiste's actions.

"She is very lovely, is she not, Your Grace?" Eleanor frowned, but the dressmaker stepped back and wagged a finger at her. "No, no, do not dispute me. Your figure is divine. We shall have the men falling on their faces to dance with you."

"They will not dance very well if they are on their faces, Celeste," the Dowager replied dryly, but she had a twinkle in her eye. "Do not worry, my dear Eleanor. Celeste is an old friend, and you are in the best of hands. She is right, you know. You *do* have a lovely figure, and Celeste will display it to its best advantage."

"I'm not sure I want to be displayed," Eleanor muttered. "I am perfectly content to hide in the wings."

"But is that what your Duke wants?" the redoubtable Madame LeRoche asked. "You are a Duchess now and must act as your rank demands. And your husband, of course."

Eleanor thought for a moment, but the woman was right. If this were the role she must play to make Jamie happy, she would do it. Even if he had been forced to this marriage, she would do all she could to help him not regret it.

Madame LeRoche swept them into the next room where fabrics in all colors were in piles on tables. Eleanor gasped at the sight, and the Dowager immediately picked up a lovely light blue brocade.

"No, no," Madame LeRoche scolded. "Not with her coloring. She needs the darker hues, vibrant colors, not a debutante's pastels."

"I'm in mourning," Eleanor said. "I should not wear colors."

The Dowager turned and put a gloved hand on the side of Eleanor's cheek. "Oh, my dear, I know that you miss your father greatly. But a new bride has some exemptions, and it has been six weeks since your father's passing. If we are careful with our selections, we can observe the conventions."

Eleanor was doubtful, but the Dowager knew the rules. She watched as the two women pulled out bolts of fabric, amicably arguing over pattern and type of cloth. Two younger women came into the room, and Madame snapped her fingers.

"Voile! Please take the Duchess into the fitting room. We must get her measurements."

The two girls hustled Eleanor off and immediately removed her dress. She was getting a little weary of being treated like a doll, but Eleanor kept her patience and let them strip her down to her chemise. One girl led her to a stool and posed Eleanor on it while the other knelt with tape and pins. The two were busily measuring and recording the numbers when Madame and the Dowager came in to see how they progressed.

Madame picked up Eleanor's discarded stays. "Oh," she moaned and held them out for the Duchess to commiserate. "It is as I thought."

Eleanor blushed, not sure what the problem was with her undergarments, but Madame was glad to enlighten her.

"Such a magnificent bosom and all stuffed into this armor, this shell. The breasts need freedom to breathe, to show their glory. This is all wrong." Madame tossed it aside. "You are not comfortable, non?"

She patted Eleanor's stomach. "We shall fix it, do not worry, Your Grace."

Eleanor objected, "I am a modest woman, Madame. I'm not sure I want my..." she motioned at her chest, "anything to breathe."

"Try it," suggested the Dowager. "Listen to Madame, Eleanor. She will not steer you wrong."

Eleanor looked at the three encouraging faces around her and nodded to the Dowager. She hoped that Jamie would like whatever it was they would do to her.

Several hours later, Eleanor was utterly exhausted. She'd been pinned and prodded on every part of her body, it seemed. Material of every hue had been held up next to her or draped over a shoulder while the other women consulted and made offensive remarks. Oh, Eleanor knew they did not mean to be offensive, but she was tired, and it was hard not to take them as such.

She could finally dress again; one assistant helped despite her insisting she could do it herself. She was more than ready to return to Carlisle House and put her feet up though the Dowager was fresh and prepared to do more shopping; she was talking about shoes, bonnets, and reticles to Eleanor's dismay.

Eleanor stepped out into the front of the shop where the Dowager was waiting for her just as another woman entered the store. She was beautiful, a little older than Eleanor, but an English rose with blonde hair and blue eyes. She was petite and dressed impeccably.

"I am here for my appointment, Madame," she announced. Her eyes widened, and she rushed over to the Dowager. "Your Grace, I didn't expect to see you here."

"Your Grace," the Dowager nodded. "Nor did I think to see you. I believed most of the Ton have left for the country."

"We will retire shortly. Thomas had a cold, and the doctor recommended that we wait until he recovered." The woman simpered at the Dowager, there was no other word for it, Eleanor thought. "How is your son? I have not seen His Grace for several weeks. Such a busy man. He had promised me a dance at the Remington's ball and then disappeared before he could claim it. An estate emergency, I believe."

Eleanor disliked this woman on sight. Who was she to put claims on Jamie? Eleanor was sure that the woman wanted more than a dance from him, the way she was talking.

"His Grace is well," the Dowager answered. "Very well indeed. Your Grace, let me introduce you to my new daughter-in-law, the Duchess of Carlisle." She turned to Eleanor, a proud smile on her face, and Eleanor stepped forward and nodded to the other woman. "Your Grace, may I introduce you to the Duchess of Chichester."

The blonde woman, also a Duchess apparently, nodded to Eleanor. Her glance swept up and down Eleanor's form, judging her instantly. Eleanor squared her shoulders, ready for battle.

"So nice to meet a friend of my husband's," she said.

The Duchess of Chichester nodded coldly. "I have not heard of you before. Which part of the country are you from?"

"I hail from Devonshire, Your Grace."

"And your family?"

"They also come from Devonshire," Eleanor answered, knowing was not the real question. "But I fear we are late for another appointment." She turned to her mother-in-law who smiled in agreement.

"Madame, we will expect to hear from you soon," she said, all hauteur with others about.

"Of course, Your Grace," Madame LeRoche answered, but she winked slyly at her old friend who stifled a grin. Apparently, Madame's spirits were irrepressible even with three Duchesses in her tiny shop.

The Dowager swept out without another word, followed by Eleanor. They did not see the Duchess of Chichester narrow her eyes as she watched them leave.

Chapter Nineteen

Jamie paced back and forth in his bedchamber, dressed for dinner, but hoping to hear Eleanor before so he could escort her downstairs and have a word or two with her along the way. He had missed her terribly today, much more than he expected when he left her sleeping this morning. She was gone most of the day with his mother shopping, and Martin had informed him she was resting when he looked for her after her return. Reluctantly, he had let her be.

Still, he felt that something was wrong since their arrival in London. He had looked forward to taking her around and showing her the sights before they retired to the country. If he hadn't had to catch up on estate matters, he would have gone with them today irrespective of that he hated shopping.

His mother had assured him that Eleanor was all right and that they had accomplished a lot. His wife would be attired suitably, and his pocket would be considerably lighter, not that Jamie begrudged the expense. He looked forward to showering more gifts on his new wife and would have liked seeing to her comfort and her being made happy with the furbelows that women enjoyed.

There was a noise from the next room, and he tapped on the door. It surprised him when Martin opened it instead of Eleanor.

"Her Grace has gone down to dinner already."

"Thank you." Eleanor could be quiet as a mouse when she chose, he thought ruefully but went to find her. His mother was always prompt, so there was little chance he would discover Eleanor alone, but just the sight of her would lighten his day.

He was right; the two women were conversing when he entered the sitting room. He was late, and dinner served almost immediately. Eleanor seemed revived, to his relief, and chatted amicably, telling him amusing observations about her day. His mother liked his wife very much though she had told Jamie that she would not interfere between husband and wife. Still, Jamie took great pleasure that the two women in his life were friendly with each other.

"Eleanor, I have news that may interest you. Mr. Phillips, my inestimable secretary, has solved our mystery of where the Baron's money has gone."

She looked up from her dinner, her eyes alert and interested. They had spent considerable time going through the books to find the missing sums while in Devonshire.

"It turns out that there was another ledger hidden inside another one we missed."

Eleanor looked excited. "Can you recover the sums for the tenants and maintenance of the estate?"

"I'm afraid not, though you shouldn't worry about that. I'd already transferred funds to reimburse those accounts, and Mr. Brown has been taking the necessary steps to utilize those monies as part of his duty as an agent." Jamie took a sip of wine, enjoying Eleanor's puzzlement.

"It turns out the Baron has been sending the sums to his daughter here in London."

"I don't understand. I did not know the Baron ever married or had a daughter. She never visited Wykeham Hall, I believe."

"She did not, and you are correct, he never married. Miss Milsham was born on the wrong side of the blanket."

The Dowager Duchess put down her spoon, her brow furrowed. "It is most unusual for a man to make settlements to support his offspring from such an affair." She tilted her head towards Eleanor. "I admire the man for taking his responsibilities so seriously."

Eleanor frowned. "It was a considerable amount of money. I would have thought he could have supported his daughter and maintained the estate rather than pass it all to her."

"It seems excessive, but the money has gone to a good cause. Miss Milsham was sent to a girls boarding school in Bath when young and found it a comfortable environment, apparently. As she reached her majority, she has founded her own school for indigent girls here in London. The money has been going to support her school."

Eleanor sat back, her mind in clear confusion. The old Baron had never shown by either word or deed he might contribute to such a charitable enterprise, at least based on his account books. Eleanor had told Jamie that the villagers judged the Baron to have a tight hold on his purse in Sourton, not one for tossing a few pennies to the local boys or buying another man an ale at the Highwayman. That he was sending his coin to support a school for young girls was just amazing to her, and Jamie liked seeing her at sixes and sevens.

"What is the name of the school, James? Do you know?" his mother asked.

"I am told it's called Lambeth School for Girls and is near the Archbishop's Palace on the other side of the river. It is an up-and-coming neighborhood, respectable and merchant class."

Eleanor was still shaking her head. "I confess, of all the options for where the old Baron invested his money, a school for girls was not at all one I would have guessed."

"Mr. Phillips did some investigation for me. Miss Milsham is known as Mrs. Milsham although she never married, but that would not be unusual for a woman in her position. Her school is well regarded, and she finds jobs for the girls as governesses or companions once they graduate. Some have found work as milliners or seamstresses."

"How intriguing," the Dowager said. "How old was the Baron when he died?"

Eleanor responded, "In the village, we called him the old Baron, but he must only have been in his fifties. He was somewhat overweight and not in good health, so he seemed older than he was."

"Then the daughter must only be around thirty years of age," the Dowager exclaimed. "She has assumed quite a responsibility for one so young."

"She is actually about Eleanor's age," Jamie smiled at his wife.

"My goodness. I don't feel able to take on the task of operating such an enterprise. How brave of her."

Jamie tilted his glass toward his wife. "You have taken on the entire operation of a duchy. How brave you are!"

Eleanor smiled, but she had a troubled look.

ELEANOR PACED BACK and forth across her sitting room, her dress swishing as she walked. The Dowager had decreed that she could not go out until some of her new dresses arrived which wouldn't be until tomorrow at the earliest. She had wandered around Carlisle House but felt in the way of the army of servants who maintained the house, busy with dusting and waxing of the already gleaming wood.

She felt trapped. Jamie could come and go as he pleased. He promised to take her out soon, but Eleanor couldn't help but think his new wife already bored him. He still came to her bed at night, but disappeared during the day, either into his office with his secretary or out of the house on different errands where she wasn't included.

Pausing to look out her window, Eleanor could see it was another rainy day. She missed the sunshine of Devonshire, the open fields and moors where she could walk without fear of anything but a wayward sheep. Here she must always have an attendant. A trip to the bookstore meant calling out the carriage before she and Martin were allowed out for the short trip. Eleanor was guarded by a footman who carried the single book she'd bought as if she were too feeble to lift the slim volume.

She watched as a governess herded a small girl down the sidewalk, her umbrella open to protect the child from the misty rain. Eleanor sighed and dropped the curtain, then turned back to resume her pacing when she had a thought. She crossed to her dressing room where Martin was busy rearranging the bonnets and reticles that had already come from Madame's shop.

"Martin, we are going out. Can you have the carriage brought around?"

Martin looked startled but was trained too well to object. Eleanor thought perhaps she might be just as ready to get out of the house as Eleanor. Martin went to summon a footman and returned to find Eleanor already buttoned into a pelisse. She wanted to escape the house before either the Dowager or Jamie thwarted her trip.

The Duke's stables were efficient, and before she knew it, Eleanor was on her way. The trip was across London, but she didn't look out at wet streets, still too overwhelmed at the idea she had left Carlisle House on her own. Martin perched on the seat across from her, brimming over with curiosity, but knowing better than to ask.

Eleanor clenched her gloved hands together in her lap. A quick glance out the window showed that the rain was abating. The carriage pulled up in front of a large building that looked relatively new.

"Your Grace," Martin asked. "Are you sure you want to go here?"

"Yes, Martin, I do. I'm curious about this school for young girls." Eleanor waited while the footman opened the door and helped her and Martin out of the carriage. She waited impatiently for the footman to rap on the door and explain to the young woman who answered that the Duchess of Carlisle was here to see Mrs. Milsham.

The young maid opened the door wider, and the footman indicated that Eleanor should enter. She smiled as she passed him, thinking she needed to learn his name. The maid led her and Martin to a sitting room. Eleanor could hear the faint sounds of talking coming from beyond the doorway where they stopped.

In just a moment, a thin woman dressed soberly with her hair pulled back demurely entered the room.

"Your Grace," she said and curtsied. "I am Mrs. Milsham. How may I help you?"

Right off, Eleanor decided she liked the no-nonsense approach that the woman displayed.

"Mrs. Milsham, I am from the village of Sourton in Devonshire."

The schoolmistress's lips tightened, but she nodded.

"I knew your father," Eleanor glanced at Martin, but the maid was studying the tips of her half-boots, seeming to ignore the conversation, but probably taking in every word. "My husband inherited Wykeham Hall from him. I'm very sorry about his passing."

"Thank you. He was a good man."

Eleanor thought they could hardly call the Baron that as he left the people of the village wanting, but she supposed that the daughter who had enjoyed his largess would scarcely complain about him. He had treated her very well.

"I would like to know more about your school," Eleanor told her. "I am interested in what you have done here with your girls."

She turned to Martin. "You may wait in..." Eleanor looked to Mrs. Milsham.

"My housemaid will show you to the kitchen. You can have tea if you wish."

Martin obediently went off with the girl who had brought them inside, and Eleanor sat which allowed Mrs. Milsham also to seat herself.

"Tell me about your school, please," Eleanor requested.

"Would you like tea, Your Grace, first while we talk?" Mrs. Milsham answered.

"No, I am happy as I am." Eleanor was excited. It had occurred to her that Duchesses could support charities. Perhaps this school would be an opportunity to involve herself in something meaningful of her own. "Please, just tell me how you started this school and why? I would like to know?"

The young woman looked puzzled. Eleanor supposed that she rarely had Duchesses invade her premises to quiz her, but Mrs. Milsham answered readily enough.

"I was fortunate to attend a good girl's school where I was educated and taught how to make a way for myself." She hesitated and added. "I suppose you know the circumstances of my birth?"

Eleanor nodded but added nothing more. There was no reason.

"My father has always been most generous with my upkeep and wanted to dower me with a large sum. We argued as I never intend to marry and wanted to use the monies to fulfill my dream of a school of my own. He finally conceded and advanced me the sums. I came to London as I felt I had a better chance here of finding girls who needed help."

"How long have you had the school?" asked Eleanor. "Forgive me, but you look young to have this responsibility."

Mrs. Milsham didn't appear offended by the question. "I *am* young for this, I suppose," she answered with a laugh. "I've had the school for four years. We have girls of all ages. The first class of graduates was this year, and I believe we found good positions that fit each young woman. I'm fortunate in that two of the older women who taught at my school in Bath came with me to teach here. They have been invaluable in helping me find my way."

"Would you show me around the school?"

A look of puzzlement passed over Mrs. Milsham's face, but she was too well-bred to demur. "Of course, Your Grace," she said as she rose. Eleanor followed her as she led her down the hall to where a classroom of young girls was laboring over their slates adding up sums. An older woman was walking around the room, occasionally stopping to point out a mistake or to help one of the girls. They did not interrupt the class, just peeked in from the hallway for a few moments.

As they walked away, Mrs. Milsham confided, "They are among our youngest. We spend most of their time on schoolwork with some play time. As the girls grow older, we incorporate more lessons in needlework, music, and art. My goal is to give these girls options. All of them will go on to work, but it should interest them if possible. We try to make our curriculum varied but practical."

They stopped at another room where some older girls were bent over their needlework projects. A few were knitting, one was tatting lace, but most were embroidering on linen.

"These girls will seek positions as governesses in a few years," Mrs. Milsham said in a quiet voice. "They continue their studies, but split their time among other pursuits they will teach to their charges such as watercolor painting or piano."

The schoolmistress continued to show Eleanor around the school until they ended up back in the room where they had initially met.

Mrs. Milsham straightened her shoulders. "Is there any other way I can help you, Your Grace?"

"I think it might be more to the point to discuss how I may help you."

Chapter Twenty

Jamie paced in the hallway, waiting for Eleanor to descend the stairs. This was the first night they would go out in public as a couple, and he was nervous. Not for himself, but for his new wife. Eleanor was tense but determined to put on a brave face. His mother was going with them, so she had the support of both of them, but this was a different world than Eleanor was used to, and it could be cruel.

He was confident his mother had seen to Eleanor's wardrobe and that Eleanor would look like the Duchess she now was. Jamie patted his pocket where the necklace he had purchased for her rested. He had ensured that Martin knew of his surprise and would guide his wife to a dress color that matched the emerald stones.

Eleanor had been patient with him. Jamie had been busier since they had come to London than he had expected and he hadn't been able to take her about as he wished. The lack of a suitable wardrobe had also hampered any excursions. Jamie did not want to embarrass her in any way, so she had only been out shopping a few times as far as he knew.

Society was leaving London for the country anyway, and the number of parties and balls had decreased significantly. Many families had already departed for their rural estates or for house parties elsewhere. He had received several invitations himself and had committed to one house party before he had left for Devonshire. Jamie was unsure that he would attend now that his circumstances had changed. Dragging Eleanor into what was often a scandalous environment might not be the best decision.

A noise alerted him that his wife and mother were coming down the stairs. The Dowager waited at the top, allowing Eleanor to descend first and display her new gown. It was a dark green satin that suited her coloring and discreet enough for a bride just coming out of mourning. The neckline framed her generous bosom and would be the perfect setting for the necklace in his pocket. The satin swished as Eleanor stepped off the last stair and then the skirts settled.

Jamie held out a hand, and Eleanor took it, a shy smile on her face. Her dark hair was up in loose curls with a green velvet ribbon entwined throughout. She looked absolutely beautiful.

"Doesn't Her Grace look lovely?" His mother had come down while he was still gaping at Eleanor.

"Extremely so." Jamie leaned forward and bussed his wife on the cheek. He reached into his pocket and pulled out the velvet wrapped parcel. "I got this for you to commemorate this occasion, the first of many." He pulled the necklace out and moved behind her to fasten the clasp after he draped the jewels around her neck.

The Dowager came around to look as Eleanor put a hand up gently to touch the stones. She held Eleanor's chin. "Perfect, both you and the necklace. I'm proud of my new daughter-by-marriage. My son chose well."

Eleanor blushed, but she beamed a happy smile. She had a flowered silk shawl hanging over one elbow, and Jamie helped her pull it up around her shoulders, squeezing gently as her lavender perfume wafted through the air. Jamie thought briefly about canceling their plans and taking her back upstairs, but he knew she was looking forward to their evening.

The butler had helped the Dowager into her cape, and Jamie took a woman on each arm. The carriage was waiting, and they were off to the opera.

Jamie had decided that this would be a proper introduction to society for his wife. A notice had been placed in the papers so it would not surprise people to hear of his marriage, though they would be eager to appraise his bride.

They were to hear one of the last performances of the season, *La Scala di Seta*, by an Italian named Rossini. Jamie enjoyed the music and the stories told in these colorful presentations. He kept a box at Covent Garden for his use when in London and he hoped that Eleanor would enjoy the excitement and what crowds there were this late in the season.

The carriage slowly followed the line of coaches until they were in front of the theater. The footman opened the door, and they descended to stand in a small cleared area on the sidewalk. There were still enough people in town to fill the theater, and Jamie led them to his box where they could oversee the people filling the seats below. Eleanor leaned forward, her attention rapt on the people all around her. She didn't seem to be aware of the many eyes that were staring at her. Jamie reached out and took her hand.

"Is it what you expected?" he asked.

She turned to him with shining eyes. "Oh, so much more. I've never seen the like."

"At intermission, we will walk around. I see some old acquaintances I would like to introduce you to this evening."

She nodded and settled back in her seat. People were sitting down as the orchestra finished tuning their instruments. Then the curtain went up, and the performance began.

Jamie ended up watching Eleanor more than the actual opera. Her wonder and absorption in the story being played out on the stage was engaging. Her eyes never left the players. The opera was a farce, noted for its comedic elements, and Eleanor found much amusement in the story. The second part of the show comprised solos and reenactments of other parts of operas. It was an excellent introduction for a neophyte. In fact, many people had brought their older children for the performance.

Intermission came, and Eleanor blinked as the audience applauded. Jamie stretched and turned to his mother.

"Will you walk with us, Mama? Or shall I bring you some limeade?"

"I think I will stay here. I see Lady Broughton waving, and she will come over to talk, so I am quite all right here as I am."

"Very well." He turned to Eleanor and winged an elbow at her. "Shall we walk around and get fresh air?"

"Yes, please," she replied with a smile. "That would be lovely."

"Have you enjoyed the vocals?"

Eleanor leaned her head briefly on his shoulder and sighed. "It is all so wonderful. The costumes, the music. I love it." She paused and tugged on his sleeve. "Thank you so much for bringing me tonight."

Her comment took Jamie aback. "It is my duty as your husband to escort you to affairs such as this."

Her face fell, and he hastily amended, "And I enjoy it very much as well. It is refreshing to see this all anew through your eyes."

More people were coming out of their boxes and wandering the halls, looking for friends to gossip with, but Jamie just nodded to acquaintances and kept walking. He didn't want to overwhelm Eleanor at this point. He murmured names to her and headed steadily toward the main lobby. It was crowded there, people in little groups of women in bright dresses contrasting with the men in black.

Eleanor was looking everywhere, the sparkling chandeliers, the gowns of the other women, not overtly, but Jamie could feel her excitement by the tension of her arm on his. She seemed unaware she was getting as many looks herself. Eleanor looked beautiful in her new gown. People had read the announcement and were curious about the new Duchess of Carlisle.

"Your Grace," a woman's voice accosted him, and Jamie paused. He knew voice though he didn't want to talk to the woman at all. He turned to see the Duchess of Chichester smiling at him, her dress as blue as her eyes and cut low to display her... assets. She nodded at Eleanor but never took her eyes off Jamie.

"Your Grace," Jamie bowed. "Please let me introduce my wife, the Duchess of Carlisle. My dear, this is the Duchess of Chichester. Lydia is an old friend from my youth."

"Oh, James," she trilled, and he felt Eleanor stiffen next to him. "I met your new wife at the modiste last week. Didn't she tell you?"

Eleanor cleared her throat. "I thought my mother-in-law passed on your good wishes."

Lydia dismissed Eleanor by turning back to Jamie and tapping her fan on his chest. "I declare, you make it sound as if we are ancient. We may be old friends, but surely not old in years." She held out her dress brazenly as if to display her charms and in truth, Lydia was still young and beautiful despite her widowhood and child.

She turned back to Eleanor. "Surely James has spoken of me to you. At one time, we thought to marry ourselves, but alas, my family made other arrangements."

Eleanor inclined her head and replied coolly, "Yes, I believe he has told me some tales of your past together." She glanced at Jamie. "And the rupture of your previous friendship."

Jamie did not allow it to show, but he was proud of Eleanor for her demeanor in the face of Lydia's insolence and rudeness. She was not allowing the other woman to threaten her poise, and Eleanor displayed more of the manner of a Duchess than the other woman with the same title.

"My dear, I believe the second part of the performance will start soon. Perhaps we should return to our box."

"Of course. So nice to see you again, Your Grace." Eleanor tilted her head, ignoring the snide look on Lydia's face. She walked along the side of him, holding onto his arm and her head held high, ignoring the looks of the gossips who had marked every bit of the meeting between the two women.

Eleanor was silent as they returned to their box. Jamie couldn't tell what she thought though he wondered why she hadn't mentioned meeting Lydia earlier. He didn't know why the woman had even bothered to approach him. She'd been widowed for two years and had never concerned herself with him before this. For her to approach tonight was bizarre, and he wanted to know why. He was sure it meant trouble.

They sat down as the curtain rose once again. Jamie watched his wife rather than the performance, but Eleanor gave nothing away. Still, he thought the enjoyment from earlier in the show had left her, and she was instead enduring the rest of the music. He felt his mother glance over a few times and knew she felt the tension in the box between them.

The ride home was quiet though Eleanor and the Dowager discussed the music and her enjoyment of the show. She expressed her thanks several times, frustrating Jamie as taking Eleanor to the opera was such a minor happenstance, and she should not feel so beholden to him for it. He wanted to do so much more for her and would if it would gain her love.

Jamie escorted her to her chamber and then retired to his own where Bates was waiting to undress him. He fussed, hurrying his valet along, wanting to get to his wife. He threw on his robe and entered her bedroom.

Martin was still there taking Eleanor's hair down.

"I can do that," he said. Jamie took the brush away from Martin and nodded for her to leave. He found a few more pins as Eleanor's dark hair fell to her shoulders. Her hair was so glossy, shades going from chestnut to dark browns. Jamie pulled the brush through a lock and let it fall. He moved his fingers into her hair, massaging her scalp underneath, and Eleanor let her head drop back with a moan that went straight to his groin.

Jamie continued to massage her head and then gently pushed her head forward as he moved to her neck and shoulders. He dropped a kiss on the nape of her neck and Eleanor moved a hand up to cover the big hand on her shoulder as she leaned her head back to rest on his hip.

"Thank you again for tonight."

"Eleanor, I don't need your gratitude. I owe you so much for agreeing to marry me and be my wife." He dropped another kiss on her other shoulder and straightened, looking at her reflection in the mirror.

"I think you guessed that the Duchess of Chichester was my former fiancee, the one who deserted me for a better catch."

"Perhaps she thought she was getting a better catch. I know that she didn't." Eleanor patted his hand, but Jamie wanted a smile from her. He had the fleeting thought his wife didn't smile much, and Jamie vowed that he would change that in the future.

"It doesn't matter. I have what truly matters right here in my arms." Jamie stooped and lifted Eleanor into his arms, then strode across the room to place her gently in their bed. For now, he knew one guaranteed way to make her smile.

Chapter Twenty-One

Martin packed Eleanor's things in her new trunks. It amazed her at how much more she was taking with her compared to when she had arrived at Carlisle House. It was wasteful to the 'vicar's daughter' part of her personality, but her feminine soul thrilled as the boxes and trunks piled up.

Eleanor was dressed in a mauve traveling gown with a matching hat, newly delivered by Madame LeRoche the day before. She picked up her reticule and left the room. They would travel to Carlisle over the next weeks, stopping for a house party along the way. Jamie had apologized profusely, but he'd agreed to the event before their marriage and didn't feel he could renege on the invitation now. His mother was continuing on to Dalemain to ready the dower house for her occupation. Both he and Eleanor had protested her removal, but she stated that she was looking forward to the change, and they couldn't change her mind.

When Eleanor reached the front hall, it was a bustle of noise as servants rushed to and fro. "I'm so sorry I'm late," she said, looking at the ado about her.

Jamie took her hand and smiled. "Not a problem. I just put Mother in the coach and came back in for you. We can escape this confusion and let Martin and Bates deal with it all."

The two servants were overseeing the packing and would follow in a coach carrying the baggage. The dowager's carriage was also following with her maid and trunks. She would ride with Jamie and Eleanor for the first part of the journey until she split off for her own trek. Eleanor had never seen such an entourage, but she supposed it was just one more thing to get used to.

The afternoon before she had secured time with Jamie and tell him of her visit to Mrs. Milsham's school. She had explained what she had found and convinced him of her interest she would like to act as a patroness for the school. Eleanor was sure that once they returned to London in the fall and met people, she might gather like-minded people to aid her.

Jamie had listened carefully, asked a few questions, and then set John Phillips to some further investigation. He also promised an initial investment in the school which made Eleanor happy. Jamie teased that it was nothing to the amount she had spent on her wardrobe which appalled her until he admitted he was just attempting to provoke her.

The journey was much as the trip to London had been. The weather was getting warmer as summer came on strong, but they were as comfortable as anyone could be in a well-sprung and luxurious coach. Jamie spent much of the trip on Ajax riding beside the carriage and Eleanor could not begrudge him the opportunity to ride in the fresh air after the weeks in the dirty air of London.

The house party was at the estate of a Lord Blakesley, or rather his parents, the Earl and Countess of Wexham. Jamie thought the object of the party was to find a wife for Lord Blakesley, who was resisting marriage. Their mutual friend, Baron Aversley, had recently married though Jamie had missed the ceremony. Aversley had sent him a letter telling him that Lady Lucilla Blount, the woman Jamie had once proposed to, had married her old sweetheart, Viscount Lovell. With all the marriages happening, it appeared that Lord Blakesley's days of freedom were ending.

At any rate, Jamie hoped that she would meet some of his acquaintances, so Eleanor was willing to accompany him for the week before they continued on to Dalemain. He wasn't clear on who would attend, but Jamie assured Eleanor that there would be numerous young ladies invited as potential brides for Lord Blakesley among others. Privately, Eleanor thought those same young women had harbored hopes for the position of Duchess of Carlisle, and she wouldn't be very popular with them, but she would reserve her apprehensions until she actually met them.

They had parted from the Dowager that morning, and Jamie was riding inside the carriage with her. Eleanor had attempted to read a book but found herself too interested in the passing countryside. Perhaps when she had traveled more, she would ignore the scenery, but for now, she found it fascinating.

Jamie was perusing paperwork, marking messily on the corners of some of the documents from his traveling desk. Eleanor didn't see how he could get any work accomplished, but she didn't disturb him or offer to help.

When he put everything back inside the desk and placed it to one side, Eleanor knew they must be close to the Wexham's estate. The coach slowed and turned through some iron gates, and Eleanor put her book on the seat and leaned forward to look out the window.

"Tell me again about Lord Blakesley," she coaxed Jamie.

"To tell the truth, I don't know him that well. Harry Wilton is from an old family, but he is a few years younger than I am." Jamie pulled at a cuff on his coat. "I was in school and friends with Richard Blount, Earl of Wakefield, and Edmund Pryce, Earl of Thornton. Blakesley, Aversley, de Vere or Lovell I suppose I should call him now, and Thornton's younger brother was a few years behind us."

"Then how did you get invited to this party?" Eleanor asked. "Or was it merely a matter of your consequence?"

Jamie looked up, startled at her remark, and relaxed when he saw she was teasing him.

"No," he laughed, "never that. I knew Richard's younger sister, Lucilla or Lucy, and Edward, Thornton's younger brother, because of my friendships with both of them. Lucy grew up with Lovell, and Blakesley and Aversley were part of their group."

He glanced out, but the driveway was a long and winding road to the house. "I like Aversley and Edward, who is Earl of Thornton now that Edmund passed away, very much. Blakesley, to tell you the truth, can be a bit of gossip." He winced. "Circumstances in my life were very different at the time I accepted the invitation."

Eleanor leaned over and patted his knee as the carriage rocked to a stop. "It's only a week," she said. "I imagine it will pass quickly. And be amusing."

Jamie grunted as the footman opened the door. He descended and turned to help Eleanor step down onto the graveled drive.

The house was sandstone, an imposing building with double doors in the front and a tinkling fountain set in a bed of flowers to one side. Green lawn spread everywhere. Judging by the length of the drive, the Earl of Wexham had a large estate.

An older man and woman were standing at the top of a small portico waiting for them. A younger man, dressed as a London dandy, stood next to them.

"The Earl and Countess of Wexham, and their son, Lord Blakesley," Jamie whispered into her ear as he led her forward.

The Earl and his wife greeted them graciously as did Lord Blakesley though his eyes lingered too long on Eleanor's bosom for her liking. She noticed that Jamie also saw his glance and stared rather pointedly back at the young man who was not as young as she thought, but perhaps her own age or slightly older. He should know better.

The Countess led them inside, holding onto Eleanor's arm as she kept up a steady stream of orders to servants and chatter about the planned activities during the house party. Lunch was to be in an hour and meanwhile, a maid would take Eleanor to her chamber so she could freshen up. The baggage coach had followed them, and servants would bring her trunk to her room.

"I was so surprised to hear about His Grace's marriage," the Countess said, her lilac perfume overwhelming Eleanor. "I had to redo my numbers of course, as I had one less eligible man in the party, but less competition for my son." She laughed and patted Eleanor's shoulder. Eleanor thought it had confirmed her suppositions about Jamie's invitation.

"We've put you in the room next to His Grace. I'm sorry that the rooms do not connect since you are newlyweds," the Countess prattled, and Eleanor blushed.

"I'm sure my chamber is lovely," Eleanor responded. The woman seemed kind, but Eleanor was seeing where her son might have inherited his penchant for gossip. The Countess was undoubtedly angling for tidbits of news.

Her room *was* lovely, spacious with a large window overlooking the back gardens. Water glinted in the distance, and Eleanor couldn't wait for an opportunity to walk out to inspect the pond for waterfowl or wildflowers she could press.

"Luncheon will be served in about an hour. Most of the guests have already arrived, and you'll meet them at the meal. We have activities planned for the next few days culminating in a ball. I hope you find them all enjoyable as many were planned exclusively for the ladies who are eager to meet you."

"Thank you. I look forward to meeting them also."

The Countess bowed out as Martin bustled into the room. She sniffed, not as impressed as Eleanor. She ordered the footmen who followed her in with the trunk that Eleanor was using for the duration of the party to place it at the foot of the bed and immediately opened it and pulled out gowns, muttering to herself all the while.

Amused, Eleanor asked, "Is there a problem, Martin?"

Her head popped out of the trunk, and she said, "Not to be speaking out of turn, Your Grace, but you should be in a suite, not that other Duchess."

"What other Duchess and how do you find out these things so quickly?"

"The Duchess of Chichester and servants talk."

Eleanor felt a momentary unease. She didn't care for the Duchess and wasn't happy to discover that she was attending the house party. Still, it was only one week.

She waved a hand in the air. "I was a late addition to the party. I'm sure the Countess had to rearrange several things."

"She had to move His Grace as well. That woman," Eleanor knew who Martin's wrath addressed, "planned to share her suite."

"Surely not," Eleanor said. "Even before his marriage, they wouldn't have put His Grace in the same set of rooms with another woman, even a widow."

"Oh, they said the adjoining doors locked, so it was as if they had two rooms, but even the servants thought there was something havey-cavey about the whole thing." Martin snapped out Eleanor's nightgown as if she were unfurling a flag, evidence of her displeasure.

Eleanor felt a lump in the pit of her stomach. Whatever designs the Duchess of Chichester might have had on Jamie dissolved with his marriage. Besides, why would the woman care about him? She had rejected him soundly years ago. She had wealth and prestige now of her own. There was no reason for her to be interested in Jamie.

Still, the sunny day had suddenly gone dim.

Chapter Twenty-Two

Jamie escorted Eleanor down to the dining hall for luncheon. As usual, he was more than ready to eat. His room was suitable and right next door to Eleanor's. The fact that he had to use the hallway to traverse to her room was an annoyance, but not the end of the world. It wasn't as if he planned to be in his room much, anyway. The Countess would have been better served to have just put them in one room together.

They walked into a crowded sitting room where people had gathered to wait for the announcement of luncheon being served. Jamie nodded to a few people he recognized but sighed with relief when he saw Edward Pryce, the Earl of Thornton, talking with Lord Blakesley. Blakeley could be all right despite his occasional frivolity, but Thornton was a genuinely sensible fellow. With relief, he led Eleanor over to where the two men were standing.

Jamie introduced Eleanor to Thornton, who looked at her with interest.

"I am delighted to meet you, Your Grace," he responded. "I congratulate His Grace on what is a sagacious choice for a bride," Eleanor smiled, and Jamie felt a flicker of jealousy. Thornton was a very handsome fellow.

Blakesley was on his best behavior for he kept his eyes at eye level. Jamie discovered the reason when Blakesley said, "I agree. His Grace has chosen well. But all these weddings are happening so quickly. First Aversley, then Lovell, now Carlisle. It's enough to make a single man tremble in his boots." He looked at a group of young ladies who were casting eyes at their small group and shuddered.

"For my part, I am well satisfied with my bride," Jamie said and clasped a hand over Eleanor's arm on his. Eleanor just smiled mysteriously, and another tremor of unease passed through Jamie. He knew she was reticent among people she didn't know well, but hopefully, she was not so unenthusiastic about her marriage.

A gong rang for luncheon, and Jamie escorted Eleanor into the dining room. The meal was casual, so he seated her next to him while Blakesley found a seat further down the table and Thornton took a chair on the other side of Eleanor. The two exchanged words again, and Eleanor laughed at something Thornton said.

While they ate, Jamie pondered his marriage. Once they had arrived in London, he had not given it much thought. His mother had Eleanor in hand, and he was busy with his own affairs. Jamie regretted that he had not spent more time with her showing her the sights of the city, but they would do that the next time they were in town.

As she continued to converse with Thornton, Jamie turned to the woman on his other side. Lady Chilton was Blakesley's maternal grandmother. She knew everyone in society and was a good conversationalist. Lady Chilton congratulated him on his marriage. Her shrewd eyes studied him as he involuntarily turned back to Eleanor at the mention of his wife.

"A love match, eh," she said.

"I, well, I suppose it is," Jamie answered slowly.

Lady Chilton patted her lips with her napkin. "I watched you with her earlier. It's all too rare among the aristocracy, especially at your rank. It must please your mother."

Jamie smiled. "My mother is very fond of my new Duchess."

Across the table, the Duchess of Chichester gave him a sweet smile. Jamie ignored her and turned back to Eleanor. Lydia had her chance with him, and now she could only look to cause trouble, though why he didn't know.

Eleanor was eating her soup, but she put her spoon down when she saw Jamie turn to her.

"I suppose I should have sat somewhere else," she said. "We are terribly unfashionable, sitting together like this."

Jamie shrugged. "I don't care. We are newlyweds. We can sit together if we like."

"Still, we should act as we mean to go on," Eleanor said with sadness in her eyes.

"Eleanor," Jamie wanted to ask her what she meant, but the footmen interrupted as they changed out the courses.

Across the table, the Duchess of Chichester gave him another one of her patented smiles, but she was staring at Eleanor and Jamie did not like the look she was giving her. He would need to keep an eye on that woman.

He would take this opportunity to spend more time with his wife. Lady Chilton had mentioned a love match. If his feelings were that obvious to the old lady, why hadn't Eleanor showed as much, or reciprocated? Jamie thought she was in love with him, but he had never asked, nor told her of his feelings. This week seemed like the perfect opportunity to find the right time and place to talk to his new wife and delve into such talk.

Unfortunately, Jamie's plan didn't work out. The Countess of Wexham had their days planned out very precisely, and much of the activities sequestered the ladies from the gentlemen. Gentlemen expected to ride out in the mornings and spend the afternoons playing pool or other manly pursuits while the women engaged in needlework, watercolor painting, and archery. The two groups came together at meals and in the evenings when there were musical entertainments or card tables set up.

Another issue was that Eleanor had her woman's monthly courses. Jamie was polite enough to let her be, not visiting her room at night even though he wanted just to hold her in sleep. But he thought she would sleep in more comfort without him in her bed.

So, once again, circumstances kept Jamie separate from his wife though this time not through his own carelessness or estate affairs, but by the house party schedule. He couldn't wait until they could leave to go to Dalemain where he could have Eleanor to himself.

His one consolation was that Eleanor seemed to enjoy herself. She was making friends with the other ladies under the guidance of Lady Chilton and the Countess of Wexham. It warmed his heart to see Eleanor talking with the other women. They admired her needlework. She was a talented artist, and though her music skills were non-existent, she enjoyed listening to others perform.

The one woman who always seemed to be able to get away from the other women was Lydia, Duchess of Chichester. Every time Jamie turned around, she was there in front of him, smiling that insipid smile and taking his arm. He hoped that Eleanor had not noticed, but if she had, she gave no notice.

Jamie was not one for games, but he would have liked to see Eleanor display a little jealousy. He was unhappy to see her often in the company of the Earl of Thornton though he suspected nothing other than that they enjoyed each other's company and that Thornton was also using Eleanor as a buffer from the other single ladies.

He walked across the lawn hoping to find Eleanor when a call stopped him in his tracks. Jamie debated pretending he hadn't heard Lydia when she hurried up to him, and he was stuck with her once again. She heaved her chest and batted her eyelashes in what she thought was an alluring manner, but Jamie was long past falling for her charms. He wondered that he ever had.

Lydia was a beautiful woman, but she couldn't compare to Eleanor's dark charms, at least to Jamie. He sighed and waited to see what she wanted this time.

"James, I was hoping to meet with you this afternoon," she said, entwining his arm with her own.

Jamie stiffened. "Your Grace, I'd find it more comfortable if you call me by my title. Carlisle will do, as I have reminded you before."

Lydia pouted, her rosebud lips in a perfect moue though something hard passed through her eyes. "But surely we are friends and friends may use familiar names with each other."

Jamie let it go for now. He wanted to get rid of her as soon as possible so he could find Eleanor.

"How may I help you, Madam?" he asked.

"I thought we could stroll together. I'm told there is a lovely path through the woods."

Jamie barely kept from rolling his eyes, but politeness won out. "Perhaps another time. I was looking for the ladies, my wife chiefly."

Lydia studied his face, weighing her options, and gave in. "They are on the side of the house. They have set archery butts up for their amusement."

"Thank you. I will find them then." He walked away, but Lydia didn't release the hold on his arm.

"I will come with you. It will interest us to watch their sporting." He almost said something at the way she said 'us' as if it meant more than it did but again let it go. Jamie had to shorten his pace to accommodate Lydia's, and he found it frustrating to have her hanging onto him.

"Your wife is charming," Lydia said, tilting her face up from under her bonnet. "She is friendly and agreeable with all. The Earl of Thornton seems particularly enamored of her."

Jamie slit a glance at the woman next to him and abruptly lost all semblance of courtesy. "Lydia, what is your game here? I am a married man, newly married to a wife I am thrilled with. Cast your lures elsewhere because they are falling short with me, and I'm finding your importunities somewhat tasteless. Forgive me for being so frank, but you have left me no other choice."

Lydia looked stunned, but Jamie knew her well and could discern that it was all pretense. Then a tear trickled down her cheek, and for a moment, he thought maybe he was wrong and had misjudged her.

"I don't know what you are saying. I did not understand my presence was so distasteful to you." She let go of his arm. "I shall remove myself at once." Lydia marched off toward where the archery party had assembled.

Jamie watched her go, troubled both by her behavior and his own. The lack of civility he had displayed appalled him, but he had tired of her being constantly underfoot when all he wanted was his wife. She made him feel uneasy. Jamie didn't trust Lydia not to cause trouble of some sort.

He followed her more slowly to where the ladies of the party had assembled for the archery contest. Many of the gentlemen had joined them, and Jamie noticed Lydia in the middle of a group, laughing with no sign of their recent altercation.

Eleanor was sitting next to Thornton. She had seen Jamie approach, but she looked away after his glance at Lydia, not pleased that he had followed the other woman to the party. She looked very distinguished in a dress of dark green with a matching bonnet tilted to one side. Thornton leaned over to say something to her, and Jamie could hear her musical laughter even as he approached them.

Just then Thornton helped her to stand, and Eleanor went to take her turn in the contest. Thornton stood behind her, too close for Jamie's liking and helped her to adjust her bow. He stepped back, and Eleanor let the arrow fly.

It hit the target just off center, not a bad shot. People clapped enthusiastically, Jamie among them, proud of his wife. Eleanor thanked

Thornton for his aid, but when she returned to the sidelines, she came and stood next to her husband.

"Bravo, my dear. That was an excellent shot," Jamie told her.

She had a small pleased smile on her face as she watched the next woman take her place. "I am not very good at this, but we practiced this morning, and I think I was not too bad a shot. At least, I didn't embarrass myself."

"You did very well. I'm proud of my wife."

The next woman let fly, just hitting the edge of the target, and they applauded her effort. Then the Duchess of Chichester took her turn, calling out to the observers, "You must be careful. I am horrible at archery, but I think I should at least try."

She stood in the lists, waiting for everyone to stop and admire her. Jamie could see no sign of hesitation, and Lydia's form looked good for someone who thought they were not very good at the sport. She pulled back the string, but at the last moment, seemed to tangle her fingers so that the released arrow flew off course, straight at where Eleanor and Jamie were standing.

Jamie didn't hesitate. He stepped in front of Eleanor, pushing her away to safety as he moved. The sting of the arrow biting into his shoulder hurt as screams broke out from the assembled crowd. Jamie reached for his shoulder, feeling the embedded arrow while Thornton held Eleanor back from reaching for him.

He bit his lip, holding back against the pain. "I think we must call a doctor," he said.

Chapter Twenty-Three

Eleanor would not leave Jamie, even when the doctor arrived and cut out the arrow. She had been the one to slice away his ruined shirt and put a pad against the wound. Fortunately, there was little blood, at least, until they had removed the arrow. Jamie lay on his stomach in his bed and only grunted when the doctor performed his surgery. He refused the laudanum the doctor left for pain, insisting it was just a minor scratch.

Eleanor knew better. Jamie was still in shock, but there was a danger that even a small wound might putrefy and go bad. And this, for all his protestations, was not tiny. The puncture was deep into his shoulder, and the doctor could not tell how much damage might have occurred. One saving grace was that it was his right arm, and Jamie was left-handed.

The doctor had bandaged the wound and put Jamie's arm in a sling. He was resting now, pale and shaken, pillows piled up behind him. Eleanor sat in a chair by his bed holding onto his other hand.

The Duchess of Chichester had been to the bedroom door, insisting on coming in to apologize to the Duke. Eleanor had Bates send her away, much to the woman's displeasure. Jamie could deal with her once he was up and about, but Eleanor wanted nothing more to do with her.

Eleanor had watched the Duchess practice in the morning with the rest of the women. In actuality, she was very skilled, and Eleanor knew the other woman would win the trifling prize that the Countess of Wexham had set for the archery contest. She supposed that the

151

Duchess's protestations of lack of talent when she stood up were merely one of her flirtation attempts.

What Eleanor really wanted to know was, had the Duchess aimed at her or at Jamie? Had the two a lover's quarrel? They had arrived separately at the lawn where the archery contest was held, but only just, Jamie following the Duchess closely.

Every time Eleanor had looked over the last few days, the Duchess was hovering about her husband. She could admit to herself that Jamie never seemed particularly happy about the woman's attention, but then Jamie was the epitome of civility and would never embarrass his wife by flaunting attentions to his mistress. If she was his mistress.

That thought had eaten away at Eleanor for the last three nights. Eleanor had her courses for the first two nights, but naively perhaps, she had thought Jamie would still share her bed. He had promised to do so after all.

Last night she'd felt better. True, she hadn't indicated to her husband that her courses had been usually light and passed quickly, but Eleanor thought Jamie might inquire of Martin as to his wife's indisposition. There had been no noise from his room she could hear though she was awake until the early hours. She wondered bitterly if he had even used his bed.

Lydia, the Duchess of Chichester, had been blunt when she pulled Eleanor aside to inform her she and Jamie had been lovers in the past and would continue to be. His marriage was not to be an impediment to their love.

That was what had hurt Eleanor the most. The woman had said Jamie loved her. He had never gotten over his youthful infatuation with her and a year ago, once she was out of mourning, they had discovered that desire had turned to passion and love.

It hurt her badly. Eleanor knew Jamie was forced into wedlock, that it had not been a marriage for love, but she had fallen in love with him, anyway. To know he gave his heart to another pained her greatly.

Lydia had said that they had seen each other in London, which explained Jamie's many absences 'on business.' He would get an heir on Eleanor, then she could retire to one of his country estates, and Lydia would act as his hostess in London.

None of this seemed like the man that Eleanor loved. Jamie had not acted this way with her in Devonshire, a man-about-town who kept a mistress and wanted a biddable wife who would not trouble him. Lydia said he planned to buy her some trinkets, a wardrobe, give her a child, and then ignore her.

While Eleanor knew this was the way of many in the Ton, Jamie had seemed different. Now her eyes were opened, and she knew what she would do. She would not make a fuss. She was the one who had trapped him into marriage, no matter how inadvertent it had been. She would do her duty. It was possible that the variation in her monthly courses meant that she was already with child. Her appetite was off, and she displayed other symptoms. Eleanor had helped deliver enough babies in Sourton to know the signs of pregnancy and even the slight flow of her courses could be a sign she was with child.

She was prepared to travel on with Jamie to Dalemain, but when they arrived, she would remove to Wykeham Hall if she was sure of her pregnancy. Then Jamie could follow his heart to the Duchess of Chichester and reconcile with her if that was what he wanted. She would nurse her broken heart in private at Sourton.

Jamie stirred and opened his eyes, but closed them almost at once. She placed a hand on his forehead which was hot. Jamie had a slight fever, not nearly as bad as when he was ill at Wykeham Hall, but still, it was not good.

Eleanor dipped a cloth into a basin of water and dabbed at the sweat on his face and chest. Then she poured a few drops of the laudanum into a glass of water and held it to his lips.

"Jamie," she said. "Wake up. You need to drink some of this." Eleanor shifted her arm under his neck to help lift his head, and he moaned, but obediently opened his mouth and gulped the water. He opened red-shot eyes as Eleanor soothed back the sweaty auburn curls from his brow.

"Don't leave me," he said.

Eleanor paused and studied his face, pondering his meaning. Finally, she gave into his pleading eyes and promised, "I won't go for as long as you want me by your side."

She wasn't sure if Jamie caught the full meaning of her answer, but his eyelids drooped, and he turned his face to the opposite side of the bed. He grunted, unable to use his right arm. Frustrated, he turned back to her.

"Lay down with me, Eleanor," he rasped. "Don't leave me."

She walked around the bed and carefully lay next to him on the bed. She was leery of jostling his injured shoulder, and she held herself tensely, but he reached across his body and clasped her hand in his uninjured left hand. Jamie's eyes closed and his breathing evened out almost immediately as the laudanum took effect.

Eleanor turned her head and watched her husband for a long while. She seldom got to study him in this manner without him knowing. Jamie's strong, masculine features weren't exactly handsome, but one didn't realize that when he was awake and in his ducal mien. Asleep, he looked younger and more vulnerable.

She wondered how often Lydia had watched Jamie in the same manner. Eleanor knuckled away a tear and tried to pull away, but Jamie would not release her hand. She did not want to wake him up again, so she resolved to wait longer until he fell into a deeper slumber.

After trying unsuccessfully twice more to get free of the bed, Eleanor had given up. It was uncomfortable trying to sleep this way, as she was mindful of Jamie's shoulder, but she was just dozing off when there was a light tap on the door.

The door swung open before she could respond. Eleanor glanced at Jamie, but the noise hadn't disturbed him.

Lydia entered the room but stopped short when she saw Eleanor.

"I didn't expect you to be here," she said in a sharp whisper.

Eleanor pulled her hand away, not caring if she woke Jamie or not but he just snorted and settled back on his pillow. She slipped off the bed and came around, stopping a foot away from Lydia.

"Let me see him!" the other woman hissed.

Her heart was beating wildly, but Eleanor forced herself to speak calmly. Some part of her wondered at the absurdity of a man's mistress forcing her way into the man's bedroom and confronting his wife.

"He has had laudanum and will not wake now." She swallowed and lifted her chin. "Perhaps tomorrow would be a better time to visit."

Lydia sniffed, but she didn't push by Eleanor to go to Jamie. If she had, Eleanor would have left the room. She wouldn't call in a footman to remove the horrid woman and have a witness her shame. Probably everyone in the house was laughing at her anyway, but she would not lose her hard-won dignity and make this even more of a farce than it already was. She sighed tiredly.

"He doesn't want you here, you know," Lydia sniped at her.

"Perhaps, but unless you want to nurse him, he's stuck with me," Eleanor replied. She waited for a heartbeat, but Lydia gave her a pleased smirk and shook her head.

She had half a mind to concede the field and let Lydia take over Jamie's care, or rather, get in Bates or someone else to watch him. She doubted the Duchess would soil her own white hands in changing bandages. Eleanor could tell that the fever wasn't severe; his constitution was strong, and he was a healthy man from what his mother had said.

"You know what?" Eleanor said. "I've changed my mind. He's all yours."

Lydia's eyes widened in shock, but Eleanor had enough of this nonsense. She never wanted to be a Duchess, anyway; all she wanted was Jamie. If he didn't want her, then she would not stand in his way. She walked through the open door and down to her room.

Martin was sitting in a corner reading a book. She put it down when Eleanor walked in, but Eleanor waved a hand dismissively. If her ladies maid wanted to read in her free time, then Eleanor didn't have a problem with it.

"Your Grace!" Martin said. "How is the Duke?"

"He'll be fine," Eleanor responded, and she bit back the burning in her throat. "But I'd like you to pack my things. I will leave here as soon as I am able and I'll need the..." She stopped, trying to decide what to call the other carriage. "I suppose it's the baggage coach. We'll leave the Duke's coach for him to use."

Martin was too well-trained to question her employer, but Eleanor could tell that she wanted to know what Eleanor was doing. The problem was that Eleanor herself couldn't answer that. She had no idea what she was planning; she just knew she needed to get out of there to a quiet place where she could think and make decisions about her future. Duchesses had some prerogatives though Eleanor wasn't sure that applied when one was leaving one's husband behind, and his rank was nominally higher. Still, she might be a country lass, but even Mrs. Hawkins had evicted her husband out of their cottage for a time after she found him kissing a young woman from the next village. Eleanor could do no less.

"Martin, would you also send a footman for the Earl of Thornton? I need to speak to him before we leave." He was the one person that Eleanor trusted with Jamie's health. He would ensure that the wound healed properly or call the doctor back if it didn't.

Martin nodded and left the room. Eleanor sat at the small desk and pulled a paper from the drawer. She needed to write a note to the Countess of Wexham explaining that she had an emergency and needed to leave, but that the Duke would stay in her care for the time being. Between the Countess, Thornton, and Lydia, she thought to herself grudgingly, Jamie should be well cared for.

Chapter Twenty-Four

Jamie woke the next morning with his shoulder on fire, and his mouth feeling like he had been swallowing the rankest gin in London. His head ached abominably. He opened his eyes and immediately closed them again, dizzy from the room swirling about him.

"Ah, he's awake, Bates. Back from the dead or better, the 'arrow of outrageous fortune.'" The voice laughed, and Jamie strained to recognize it. "Let's give him a cup of cool water and see how His Grace is feeling."

He squinted, opening an eye just enough, and found Thornton leaning over his bed, Bates hovering behind him. "What are you doing here?" he croaked.

Thornton sat back, satisfied that Jamie was awake. "The real question, my friend, is what are *you* doing?"

Bates took that opportunity to tip a cup to Jamie's lips. The water was an immense relief to his sore throat, and Jamie gulped it down. He was conscious of his nudity under the sheets and the bandages wrapped around his arm and torso. He moved his shoulder and while sore, it seemed to flex without undue pain.

"Where is my wife?" Jamie rasped. His memories of the night before were foggy from the laudanum, but he was sure that Eleanor had been sleeping with him. Had she fled when Thornton appeared? Jamie much preferred having Eleanor with him than Thornton though he didn't want her to have to do any more nursing of him. There had been enough of that in their short time together.

He looked up, realizing that neither Thornton nor Bates had answered his question. He also realized that his bladder was full and the need to empty it was urgent, so he swung his legs to the side of the bed and slowly pushed himself to standing. Bates started forward to help him, but he motioned him off and disappeared behind the privacy screen. If Thornton insisted on staying in his bedroom, then the man would have to bear with Jamie's nudity and his response to nature's call.

Once finished with his business, Jamie came out to find Bates holding out his favorite banyan. They got it over his injured shoulder without jarring it, but, truth to tell, Jamie was ready to sit again, not quite as recovered as he wished. He walked over to the chair by the fireplace and sat with a wince.

Thornton still hadn't said a word, but he nodded to Bates, who slipped out the door. Then he came and sat across from Jamie.

"I hope he's going for my breakfast. I didn't get to eat last night." Jamie tried to sound casual, but he couldn't eat if Bates brought back a tray. His stomach was roiling in uneasy knots. Something was very wrong this morning.

"Your Grace," Thornton asked, "are you going to call me out?"

Shocked, Jamie pushed back in the chair and slammed his shoulder. He took a deep breath and rubbed cautiously until the pain had ebbed.

"Do I need to call you out?" he asked carefully. "What reason do I have to duel with you, Thornton?" His hand was clutching the arm of the chair until the knuckles turned white. He dreaded what the Earl might say. He would not believe Eleanor had been unfaithful to him, but what else could Thornton mean?

"I'm afraid that you will see a reason once I've said my piece to you." Thornton pulled at his cuff and looked up at Jamie. Something in Jamie's face caused his brow to furrow, and Jamie lost his temper.

"Spit it out, man!" he said. "If my wife has fallen in love with you, then I tell you right now you may not have her. She is *my* wife, and I love Eleanor. I will win her back from you." He was roaring by the time he was done, his Scots temper on full display. Thornton's flying eyebrow had risen even higher.

"And if you've touched her, I *will* call you out," Jamie hissed, leaning forward in his chair as if ready to leap at his erstwhile guest.

Thornton leaned forward, his honor offended by the accusation. The two men looked like they might come to fisticuffs.

"Your wife has been faithful to you," Thornton bit off the words as he spoke. "It is you, sir, who have transgressed."

"Me?" Jamie couldn't believe his ears. "I have *not*! How can you accuse *me*?"

Thornton sniffed and sat back. "Do you deny that the Duchess of Chichester was in your bed this morning when I entered the room? I had to throw her out bodily to speak to you."

"WHAT?" Jamie jumped to his feet, ignoring the pain of his wound. "No, that cannot be. Eleanor was with me when I fell asleep last evening."

Thornton rose in one smooth movement. "Do you deny that you have been having a long-term affair with her? That you plan to get your wife with child and send her away so you can continue to embarrass her by your mesalliance with the Lady Lydia?"

"No, no, I don't know what you're talking about." Jamie was sure he was still hallucinating from the laudanum. Based on the history between Lydia and himself, no one could believe they were having an affair. Surely, Eleanor knew him better than that?

Thornton stayed standing, but a frown appeared on his face. Jamie's confusion and anguish were apparent. He had never been a man good at dissembling. Thornton spoke, measuring his words, "I wondered. While I have only known your wife a short time, I know Lucy well. I could not believe you would have been courting her while carrying on with another woman."

Jamie rose in a rush, ignoring the stab of pain in his shoulder. He roared at Thornton. "I should call you out for even suggesting such a thing. I have barely spoken to the Duchess of Chichester over the past several years. She appeared at this house party and has been more of an irritation than anything else." He heaved out a deep breath, trying to hold on to his temper. Thornton was a reasonable fellow, so why would he think such things?

A sudden sick feeling struck him, and Jamie sank back into his chair, his mind reeling. If Thornton thought such things, what did Eleanor think? And where was his wife?

He pushed himself erect again while Thornton eyed him cautiously and turned to the door only to halt when he heard the other man ask, "Where are you going?"

Jamie grimaced and looked down at his robe. It was extremely inconvenient that the only connection to his wife's room was through the hallway where anyone might see him. He conceded, "I suppose I should get dressed first. Ring for Bates, would you, please?"

"Your Grace, where were you going?" Jamie looked around in surprise, both at the use of his title and the repetition of the question.

"I will find my wife," he huffed. "What the devil is wrong with you, Thornton? Surely you understand that whatever lies that woman has been spreading about me, they are not true. And if Eleanor has heard even a whiff of that poison, it must upset her. I need to explain..."

Thornton interrupted, "The Duchess left the house party early this morning."

"Eh," Jamie grunted. "Well, that's good, though I would like to have confronted her to find out what the deuce she meant by all this."

"No, Carlisle, not that Duchess." Thornton had two bright red spots on his cheeks, giving him a feverish appearance to Jamie's eyes. Then he absorbed what the man had just said.

"Pardon, I'm not sure I understand," he said slowly. "Which Duchess has left the premises?" He swallowed hard, already knowing the answer in his heart while not taking it in his mind. Jamie shook his head, setting off another dart of pain in his shoulder. Suddenly, he couldn't breathe. That Eleanor had left him without a word... Jamie crumpled to the floor as Thornton tried to stop his fall too late. His head hit the leg of the chair, and he knew only blackness.

JAMIE AWOKE SOMETIME later, his head and shoulder throbbing. He vaguely remembered Thornton and Bates getting him back into his bed and Thornton administering more laudanum despite his protests. At least they hadn't called the doctor again, he thought, though he wasn't entirely sure of that fact. He kept his eyes closed, ashamed of his behavior and steeling himself to face Thornton, who he could sense in the chair by his bedside.

The door opened, and footsteps halted when they reached his bed. He was tempted to look, but waited, trying to breathe normally like a sleeping man.

"How is his Grace?" The Countess of Wexham whispered, but Jamie could hear her clearly.

"Still sleeping," Thornton answered. Jamie twitched, almost giving himself away as it confirmed his supposition. "I expect he will wake soon."

"Is there anything I can do, my lord? I can have a maid come to sit with him and give you some respite."

"No, that is very kind, but I think the Duke would be more comfortable with his man or me. The wound to his head bled profusely, but was very minor."

"I wish the Duchess hadn't been called away." The Countess sounded worried. "Are you sure we should not send for her?"

"Before his fall, the Duke was quite clear it was more important for his wife to visit her sick friend." Jamie huffed in surprise at the lie, but then let out a snore to cover his lapse. "Er, as I said, the Duke's head injury is not severe, and I'm sure he will be up and about, ready to join his wife shortly. It was just a bout of dizziness that felled him earlier."

Jamie heard Thornton moving toward the door, encouraging the Countess to leave. He must know Jamie was pretending sleep and was now trying to get her out of there.

"My lord, the Duchess of Chichester has been asking about the Duke." The distaste in the Countess's voice was clear. "She is insistent that she speak with him."

"Yes," Thornton answered. "She's been to the door, but I have kept her away. I'm sure that the Duke doesn't wish to see her at present and will let her know when... if he desires her company."

What the devil? Jamie thought. *Hasn't that woman caused enough trouble? What could she want with him?* Hearing the door close, he opened his eyes and struggled to sit up as best he could against the pillows. He ignored the pain in his shoulder but grunted as Thornton came back to the bed and silently piled more pillows behind him.

Jamie gratefully took a drink from the water glass offered to him, then tentatively put a hand up to his forehead. He encountered a pad of linen which explained the ache in his head. Between the wound and the laudanum, it was no wonder he felt miserable.

Thornton pressed him back against the pillows, pushing on his good shoulder, but Jamie couldn't relax.

"Where is my wife?" he demanded. "What sick friend called for her to visit without her telling me she was leaving?"

Thornton set his mouth in a mulish line. "Perhaps you can first tell me exactly what is going on with you and the Duchess of Chichester? Then I can best judge what I should reveal to you of your wife's plans."

Jamie stared at him in disbelief. Had he so unmanned himself with his faint that Thornton felt he could order him, the Duke of Carlisle, about as if he were a stable boy? His world was upside down, and he felt as if he were going mad. Still, the most important thing was Eleanor.

"Nothing is going on between the Duchess of Chichester and me. I have barely spoken to her over the last years. At one point, in my youth, we were briefly betrothed, but she jilted me for the man she married."

He glared at Thornton, ready to fly off the bed at him if he accused him further. "I am not, nor would I ever have an affair with her. Not with any woman. I believe in the sanctity of my marriage vows and am quite satisfied with my wife."

Thornton leaned back in his chair and studied Jamie. "Satisfied, Carlisle? Is that all there is between you and your lady?"

Jamie grimaced, uncomfortable with Thornton's question. He loved his wife and had almost from first knowing her, but was between the two of them. Though come to think of it, he had never said so to Eleanor. He shifted in the bed, uneasy at the thought. He looked up at Thornton's knowing look.

"Very well," Thornton said with a smirk, "let me tell you what your wife confided to me. I believe you have been ill-used, and I will divulge her secrets to aid you in this matter."

Chapter Twenty-Five

By the next day, Jamie was much recovered. He was eager to follow Eleanor, but he and Thornton had made a plan, and he wanted to resolve whatever Lydia was scheming before he left. Bates helped him dress while Thornton sought the Duchess of Chichester to meet Jamie in private in a salon downstairs.

When he was ready, he made his way carefully down the stairs. There were a few servants about, but most of the house party had departed on a walk to nearby ruins for a picnic. Thornton had assured him that the Duchess did not plan to attend the walking party, and he would ensure that she met with him in private.

The room appeared empty when he entered. Jamie noted the high-backed chair placed at an odd angle near the fireplace and deducted that Thornton had secreted himself there. It was far enough away he could not hear much, but allow him to act as a chaperone if the Duchess took things too far.

Jamie was irate once he had heard Thornton's tale of Lydia's behavior with Eleanor. That she would upset his wife with such vicious falsehoods made him want to strangle the witch. He wished that Eleanor had come to him so he could have assured her of his devotion, but after consideration, he could understand her diffidence.

In the time he had spent lying in his chamber yesterday, Jamie thought about his wife quite a bit. Reflecting on the brief period of their marriage, he realized that perhaps he had not communicated as well as he could have with her. Eleanor was equally reticent with him. He could understand that she might not want to take the lead to interact with him, but he feared she had felt forced to marry him and didn't love him, which had led to the present contretemps. If he had been more open and dared to assert his tender feelings, Eleanor might have confided in him rather than fleeing the field.

Jamie sighed, worried about his marriage and his wife. Once he found her, he would state in unequivocal terms his feelings toward her and let the chips fall where they may. He hoped that Eleanor still felt fondly towards him, but he worried that Lydia's tales might have made inroads against those sentiments. Jamie had work to do on his marriage, and he had never been one to shirk hard labor.

The door to the room pushed open, and Lydia entered. She looked delicate and pretty, her hands spread out as she rushed toward him, but it didn't impress Jamie. He much preferred Eleanor's classic looks than the false appearance of this porcelain doll.

"James. I am so happy to see you up and about." She tried to embrace him, but Jamie stepped away and lowered his chin, his eyes cold.

"What's this? I have been so worried about you," Lydia exclaimed, hands fluttering as she studied his face.

"Enough, Lydia. I want to know what you are up to," Jamie demanded.

Lydia blinked her eyes. "Why James, I have only tried to bring about what you and I both wish. What we have both wished for these last ten years."

"And what do you think that is, Lydia?" His tone was cold, but she didn't seem to notice much. She was too concerned with concocting her story.

"Why, to be together, of course." She tried to move closer to him, but Jamie shook his head and crossed his arms across his chest as best he could with the sling.

"Is that why you told my wife we had been having an affair? That we meant to continue to see each other?"

Lydia bit her lip and peered up at him from under her eyelashes, trying to look innocent and failing utterly in Jamie's eyes.

"Well, I had hoped that once I was through my period of mourning, we would find each other again."

"That was three years ago, Lydia." Jamie didn't bother to remark he wouldn't have been interested, regardless. She had not tried to attract his attention in that time; they had barely spoken since she jilted him. And he was all right with that as the status of their relationship.

"Yes but you've been busy and not always in London." She twisted her fingers together. "But what does it matter now, my love? We can be together and indulge in what we wish." She blushed prettily and looked away, but Jamie wasn't fooled.

"What is it you wish then?" Jamie asked, raising an eyebrow.

"Why you're so wealthy, we can do anything we want," she said with a wave of her hand. She looked across the room and bit her lip again, but Jamie was getting to the crux of the matter.

"Money?" he exclaimed. "You need my money? Didn't your husband leave you set up after his death?" It was making a strange sense now. Lydia needed coin and thought him an easy mark.

Lydia flounced to the sofa and sat, then nervously rubbed at her skirt. "My brother-in-law controls the estate," she said after a moment. "I have a pitiful allowance. Surely you wouldn't mind advancing a loan with appropriate... payment."

She fluttered her eyelashes, and Jamie felt sick. She was no better than a courtesan, selling her body to the highest bidder. Lydia must have been desperate to come to him for coin. And she had sorely underestimated him.

"Where did your allowance go? The dressmaker or the gaming tables?" he asked bluntly.

Lydia frowned, realizing that her game was up, and Jamie was on to her schemes. She answered sullenly, "The tables. I went to the hells with my brother, Charles, but he has no money to cover his own debts, much less mine. Now they are after me for repayment, and I am desperate."

"Not very flattering, Lydia." She shrugged and looked away. Jamie thought for a moment. It would be easy to give her the money just to have her go away, but there was no guarantee that she wouldn't be back to cause more trouble once she found herself in debt again. "How much do you owe?"

She named a sum, large enough, but not as much as Jamie feared.

"You should go to your brother-in-law and ask for an advance on your allowance. Or perhaps you could sell some of your personal jewelry."

Lydia looked at him with scorn. "Don't you think I've tried that? Most of my jewelry is paste since John took back the ducal pieces into his custody. I can't ask John for an advance. He'll shut me up in the dower house, and I shall die of boredom."

"I'm afraid that I can't help you, Lydia. Find a free man who will marry you and support you or go to John and confess all." Jamie heaved a sigh of relief. He could go to Eleanor now and explain what Lydia had been up to. Hopefully, she would accept his apologies and take him back.

"Oh, no," Lydia said as she stood and strode over to him. She plucked at his good arm trying to move it away and finally gave up. She poked a finger at his chest instead. "If you don't give me the money, I'll tell your wife we are still together. We've been in here alone for a goodly time, and I made sure that the Countess of Wexham knew that we had an appointment. No one will believe that we are not having an affair, and I will spread it throughout the Ton — unless you give me the money."

She whirled as Thornton rose from his chair and spoke, "I'm afraid, dear Duchess, that you are mistaken. You have not been alone, and I can testify to that fact." He came to stand by Jamie, who was enjoying the shock displayed on Lydia's face. "In fact, I can testify to your entire scheme since you were so kind as to lay your cards on the table, so to speak."

Lydia gasped, her hand at her chest and the color drained from her face. Jamie was happy to see the harpy dismayed by Thornton's appearance. She had no idea of his presence in the room.

Thornton continued, "I know your brother-in-law, John, quite well. I believe I should drop a word into his ear. I'm sure it would concern him that your son, the young Duke, not be embarrassed by your gambling."

Lydia's eyes welled with tears; she turned and ran from the room. Jamie watched her go, glad to be done with her and her schemes. Now he could go after Eleanor.

"Will you really speak to John?" Jamie asked Thornton.

"I believe I will," he answered. "John is a reasonable man, not nearly the ogre she made him out to be. I suspect that a spell in the country would do the Dowager Duchess of Chichester good and perhaps teach her a valuable lesson."

"She always was spoiled," Jamie mused. "I didn't realize it until after she broke our engagement, but it was a lucky thing for me when she jilted me."

"Your wife is worth ten times of her," Thornton agreed.

A twinge of jealousy went through Jamie at his words, but he ignored it. Thornton had helped both himself and Eleanor this week, and he owed the man. "I thank you for your help. While I knew Lydia was spoiled, I did not understand how spiteful she was. That she would tell Eleanor those lies rather than just asking me for a loan... well, I might have aided her if she had chosen a different path."

"Are you leaving now?" Thornton asked. "Your Duchess has had a good two days start."

"Yes, Bates has all ready for an immediate departure." Jamie grimaced. "I would like to have ridden as I could make better time, but I fear that at least for today I must follow orders from the Countess of

Wexham and stay inside my coach. Otherwise, I don't believe she'll let me depart." He laughed, suddenly feeling lighter now he had resolved at least some of his difficulties. "It's a sad day, Thornton when a Duke must kowtow to the ladies."

"Your lady is well worth the effort, Your Grace. The Duchess of Carlisle is a rare woman. I only hope to find one similar when it is my turn for the parson's noose." Thornton was somber, and Jamie looked at him in surprise. He supposed that it was time for Thornton to be looking for a spouse and to get some heirs on her.

He shook the man's hand and turned when Thornton stopped him once more.

"She said she would go to Dalemain, but I thought her manner evasive. If you don't find her there, look to your estate in Devonshire. I believe she might return to a place familiar to her."

Jamie nodded and left to bid his hostess farewell. He would untangle the mix-up with Eleanor and then they would go about creating heirs of their own.

Chapter Twenty-Six

Eleanor walked out the front door of Wykeham Hall ready for her morning ride. She had been making steady progress in her attempts and had gained confidence in her equestrian abilities. With the help of young Will as her groom, she had been taking short rides in the park, never going above a trot, but expanding her skills nonetheless.

It had been over a week since she left the house party at the Wexham estate and she had not heard from Jamie. She had hoped he might follow her and tell her that everything the Duchess of Chichester had said was wrong, that he only wanted her, and could not live without her. Perhaps she was overwrought, but she knew now for sure she would have Jamie's child, and Eleanor desperately wanted him to be with her so she could tell him the news. She feared if she sent him a letter, he would feel he had done his duty by her and be off to London with his paramour.

She had gone over and over it in her head, and Eleanor still had doubts that Jamie could be so deceptive. But the Duchess had been so assured though about their arrangement. At the thought of Jamie and *that woman* together, Eleanor's stomach roiled. Nausea had reduced her to dry toast in the morning, but even during the rest of the day certain scents or thoughts could make her queasy. Any contemplation of the Duchess of Chichester immediately made her gorge rise.

Eleanor pushed her thoughts away and smiled at young Will, standing ready to assist her into her saddle. Though Will couldn't speak, she had known him for a long time and liked the young lad very much. She was grateful for his silence during their daily rides;

Mrs. Makepeace meant well, but she and Martin both worried about Eleanor, and it wore on her.

She urged her mare to walk on, and she and Will started down the gravel driveway. The horses ambled along in the bright sunlight. Eleanor immediately felt better, breathing in the clear air of her home countryside. She determined not to be sad on such a beautiful day, or at least, not display her melancholy to the world.

They turned off to cross the park near the bottom of the drive. The horses moved so slow that Eleanor had to urge Daisy, her mare, not to crop the tall grass as they passed through. She picked up the pace slightly, and Will followed on his big gray gelding. His horse secretly frightened Eleanor though she tried not to show it. Jamie's horse, Ajax, was also a large animal, but gentle as a lamb and much better trained than Will's horse.

The animals had almost reached the copse of trees where they usually stopped, then turned around for the short ride back to the barn. It wasn't much exercise for the horses, but Eleanor often attempted a trot on the return ride.

A hawk flew out from the trees and struck near Daisy's feet as a brown hare darted between the mare's legs. The bird flew off as its prey escaped, but it had done the damage. Daisy reared, and Eleanor lost her balance, tumbling to the ground. She hit with a thud, her breath knocked out of her and stunned by the suddenness of the fall. Dimly, Eleanor knew Will had grabbed her mare by the reins and was struggling to hold the two beasts away from where she lay. She should rise and help him, but first, she needed to ensure that all her limbs still worked.

The ground thundered beneath her, and she thought she heard her name, but Will was dumb, unable to speak from birth. He could make sounds but not form words. She closed her eyes and concentrated on regaining her own speech by inhaling air into her lungs.

"Eleanor! Eleanor! Speak to me!" Jamie was here. Jamie had come for her.

Eleanor opened her eyes to see his dear face looming over her, frantic in his fear for her. He knelt and gathered her into his arms. "Are you hurt? Dear God, why were you out riding without me? Please let nothing have happened to you." He was patting her arms and legs in a most immodest fashion, and Eleanor would have blushed, but she was so glad he was here that she could pay no mind to social mores. She reached up and placed a hand on his cheek, and he stilled, partially assuaged by her gesture. His blue eyes still looked worried, but there was something else there as well. Had he come to tell her that their marriage was over? Her mind leaped immediately to the worst possible answer.

Before she could squawk, Jamie lifted her into his arms and started to walk. Will had calmed her mare and had the horse by the reins as well as Ajax. Eleanor was breathing almost normally now, and aside from feeling jarred, she knew her only injuries would be bruises on the morrow.

"Put me down please," she asked. "I'm fine to walk."

Jamie shook his head and kept going, his face grim.

"Your Grace, please. I'd rather walk."

He stopped short and put her down. "Your Grace?" He crossed his arms over his chest. "Are we back to that again?"

Eleanor tilted her face down, refusing to look at him. The fall had mussed her riding habit, and she brushed at the dirt with a gloved hand when she suddenly remembered that she was with child. She placed both hands on her abdomen and lifted wide eyes to Jamie.

"Eleanor, are you in pain? What is the matter?" Jamie saw her panic and responded, picking her up again and starting toward the house at a run.

"No, no. I think I'm all right. But I'm with child," she sputtered, struggling to get down again though she loved feeling his arms around her.

Jamie stopped and wheeled around. "Will, leave those other horses and go to fetch the doctor at once."

"No," Eleanor fussed. "I'm sure I'm fine. Please don't bother."

Jamie walked again, his strides long. Looking over Jamie's shoulder, Eleanor saw Will riding down the drive at a gallop. She sighed. She had hoped to hide her condition a while longer if it would keep Jamie with her. Perhaps it was better this way. He could return to London immediately, knowing he no longer had to present a false facade to her.

Despite her protests, Jamie carried her right upstairs past astonished servants and into his room where he laid her on his bed. Eleanor's heart fluttered at the idea he hadn't taken her to her own room, but she calmed herself, knowing this was probably just a mistake on his part. Or perhaps he didn't even intend to stay the night. She turned her face to the wall away from him where he sat on the edge of the bed.

He took her hand, and Eleanor swallowed, but she refused to look at him. Better this way than he saw her tears. She had some pride left.

"Eleanor," Jamie said and tugged at her hand. "Love, look at me."

She pressed her eyes closed tight for a moment, overcome by the endearment but then turned toward him.

He smiled at her tenderly. "I have so much to say to you. Things I've should have told you long ago."

Eleanor tried to pull her hand away. This was it. He would confess his love for the Duchess and leave her, happy to have gained an heir.

He refused to release her hand but shook his head at her stubbornness. "I am delighted to hear of the child, but I still want the doctor to examine you. I saw your fall, and while it didn't look dangerous to me, I want assurances as to your good health."

Eleanor nodded. Of course, he wanted the mother of his child to be healthy. At least he didn't seem disappointed that the fall hadn't killed her so he could marry his mistress, she thought dramatically. She had wondered why he hadn't married the Duchess before he met her. There had been the opportunity, but perhaps there was some other impediment. Oh dear, her mind was a muddle and her feelings all over the place as a result of the pregnancy. She was usually so sensible.

She looked up to see Jamie studying her expression, a frown on his brow. Eleanor looked away and muttered, "Yes, I'm sure that all is well. You may return to London, and I will send word when the child is born. I would much prefer..."

"You would prefer that I leave you here?" Jamie was caressing her fingers, and Eleanor could hardly think. "Well, I would prefer to stay with you by my side always. How could you think I would ever have anything to do with that harpy or indeed, any other woman when I have you as my wife?" He tipped her chin up, so she was forced to look at him.

"I love you and only you. I have almost since I met you."

Eleanor gasped, and her stomach whirled, its contents no longer content to stay where they belonged. The basin that Martin usually left for her was in her room, but there was a wash basin on a stand in the corner. "Please, I need the basin." She covered her hands over her mouth as Jamie scrabbled for the bowl and got it under her chin just in time. She wasn't too sick, just enough to embarrass her, but Jamie tenderly helped her and found a damp cloth to wipe her mouth after. He helped her lay back against the pillows on the bed.

"I'm so sorry. It's been sometimes happening, but it will pass as the child grows."

"It's all right, love." Jamie smoothed a loose curl away from her forehead. "I will take excellent care of you."

"But.." Eleanor sputtered. He had told her he loved her, and she had responded by asking for the basin. She was a mess. "The Duchess. I thought..."

"Never." Jamie shook his head. "It was all lies, blackmail to pay off her gambling debts. I'll explain to you later, but first, I want to be very clear. You are my dear wife. I love you. I understand that you don't reciprocate the feelings, especially after going through that deceit, but I will use every advantage I have to bring you round so you might find the affection once more that you've lost by this incident. At least, I believed you had some affection for me, and I hoped to have you love me someday as I love you."

"I *do* love you." Eleanor blurted out and blushed. "I was angry and hurt, but I have never stopped loving you. I thought you only married me because you were forced into it and then she said..." She broke off.

"Never mind what she said," Jamie responded fiercely. "She never had my heart. Only you." He gathered her into his arms for a sweet kiss interrupted by a knock on the door. The doctor had arrived.

ELEANOR AND JAMIE RETURNED to Dalemain and stayed for the birth of their first child, a son and heir named Charles after Jamie's father. He was soon followed by several brothers and sisters, but only Charles had Jamie's auburn hair which his mother insisted was an advantage for the son of a Duke. Charles wasn't so sure, but that's another story.

Don't miss out!

Visit the website below and you can sign up to receive emails whenever Jerusha Moors publishes a new book. There's no charge and no obligation.

https://books2read.com/r/B-A-LAIH-ZRKW

BOOKS 2 READ

Connecting independent readers to independent writers.

Also by Jerusha Moors

The "A" Word Romances
Abandon
Advantage
Admiration
Always

Standalone
The Handkerchief

Watch for more at www.antrimcycle.com/search/label/
Jerusha%20Moors.

About the Author

Jerusha Moors grew up in Connecticut but currently lives in Portland, Maine. Her sister introduced her to the books of Georgette Heyer and she never outgrew her love of romance novels, especially from the Regency period. She hopes you enjoy her stories and books about that period and follow her on social media. Facebook: facebook.com/JerushaMoors/

Read more at www.antrimcycle.com/search/label/Jerusha%20Moors.